NOW OR NEVER

The sound of battle was closer and Mahoney could see explosions and flashes of small firearms in the woods. That's where the Americans were, and he assumed that the Germans were a few hundred yards beyond them. He could see tanks rumbling around and shooting at each other in the distance.

"Oh, this fucking war," he growled as he tucked his head down a few inches. He didn't know when he'd screw a woman again or when he'd eat a hot meal. He might even be killed in the next five minutes. The Germans back in those hills could see him through binoculars and could call an artillery strike on him if they wanted to.

As Mahoney finished his candy bar and relit the stub of his cigar he had only one thought on his mind: He had to get back to his men—alive . . .

THE SERGEANT
#2
HELL HARBOR

BY GORDON DAVIS

ZEBRA BOOKS

KENSINGTON PUBLISHING CORP.

ZEBRA BOOKS

are published by

KENSINGTON PUBLISHING CORP.
21 East 40th Street
New York, N.Y. 10016

Printed in the United States of America

ONE

The sound of shellburst and small firearms could be heard in the distance. Master Sergeant Clarence J. Mahoney sat propped against a tree in a small forest beside a road. He was six foot two, huskily built, and wore French civilian clothes. A black beret sat low on his forehead and he chewed the unlit stub of a cigar. Bandages were tied around his left thigh, where he'd been shot three days ago in the French town of Rouget. He'd been hiding there with some *maquis,* when an SS Panzer battalion showed up. He'd stopped a bullet during the ensuing battle, but it wasn't the first one he'd stopped and he doubted whether it would be the last.

Corporal Edward Cranepool, also in French civilian clothes, was on his knees behind a bush, peering through binoculars at the road. Leduc and Baudraye, two of the *maquis,* were opening their haversacks and taking out bread, cheese, and wine. They uncorked the wine and placed the bread and cheese on Baudraye's jacket.

"Time to eat," Leduc grunted.

In a crouch, his fingers nearly touching the

ground, Cranepool moved silently toward the food, sitting beside Mahoney. Cranepool was twenty years old, tall and lithe, with straight blond hair.

"How're you feelin', Sarge?" Cranepool asked.

Mahoney ignored his question. "You see anything out there?"

"No."

Mahoney threw the cigar butt over his shoulder and reached for the bottle of wine. His leg didn't bother him too much and he could get around on it fairly well, but he couldn't move quickly. In Rouget he'd radioed his headquarters in England and reported that he'd been hit, and they said he should try to make it back to friendly lines, since he'd be a sitting duck for the Gestapo if he hung around France any longer.

It was the 9th of June, 1944. Mahoney had been shot on the morning of the Normandy Invasion. He'd been in France for three months, working with the *maquis*. Now England told him that the beachheads were secure and supplies were pouring in. It appeared as though the Germans would not be able to push the Allies out. But Mahoney knew that anything could happen in war. He'd fought in North Africa and Italy before being parachuted into France, and had tasted both victory and defeat. He'd seen friends get shot down right beside him. He was not at all sure that he'd survive the war.

Leduc chewed a piece of bread and looked at his map. "We are only about ten miles from Carentan," he said.

"They're gonna be awfully long miles," Mahoney said, slicing off a slab of cheese with his knife.

"We'll make it, Sarge," Cranepool said optimistically.

Mahoney grunted. Sometimes he got tired of Cranepool's Pollyanna bullshit, but Cranepool had saved his ass after he'd got shot two mornings ago, and Mahoney didn't feel up to screaming at him just yet.

"I hear something," Mahoney said.

Cranepool perked up his ears. "I don't hear anything."

"Go take a look."

"Okay, Sarge."

Cranepool crawled off with his binoculars, and Mahoney munched the cheese. It was genuine Port du Salut and smelled like dogshit, but Mahoney thought it was marvelous. The wine wasn't bad either, and the bread—well, he'd never known how good bread could be until he'd come to France. He wished he could relax and enjoy the meal, but his leg ached and they were behind German lines. They had to stay alert and be ready to move out at a moment's notice.

Cranepool came back, his binoculars in his right hand. "It's a German column, Sarge."

"How big?"

"Can't tell yet. I could see a lot of trucks, or maybe they were tanks."

"We'd better finish with chow before they get here."

They wolfed down the food, passing the bottle around until it was empty. All the cheese disappeared, and most of the bread. Leduc wrapped the leftovers in cheesecloth and dropped them into his haversack. They all wondered when they'd eat again.

They got down on their bellies with their captured German submachine guns and peered through the summer foliage at the approaching column. The ground was wet from recent heavy rainfall and Mahoney could feel the dampness through his clothes.

The column rumbled closer. Mahoney took the binoculars from Cranepool and looked at it. There were eight personnel carriers coming along at a pretty fast clip, on their way to the front lines to reinforce German troops already fighting there. Mahoney had seen numerous small German units like this moving toward the front during the past few days. He imagined that they were giving the Allied armies little rest.

The column passed in front of them, splattering mud and stones on both sides of the road. Mahoney looked through the binoculars into the rear of the trucks and saw the soldiers sitting on the benches, their rifles between their knees and their heads down, trying to cop a little sleep. Probably they didn't want to fight a war any more than Mahoney did, but somehow they all were in France trying to kill each other.

Mahoney lay still and watched the column move toward the horizon in the direction of Carentan. There must be a helluva battle going on if it could be heard this far away. Part of Mahoney wished he could be in it, because there was something about the chaos and violence of the front lines that he liked, and another part of him wished he was back in New York, his home town, drinking beer at the bar on the corner with his old friends, or maybe going to one of those whorehouses on Eighth Avenue.

The column was far away now, and Mahoney got to his feet with the help of his cane. "Let's move out," he said.

He slung his submachine gun over his shoulder and hobbled toward the road. Cranepool and the two *maquis* followed him, looking cautiously about them. They reached the road and began walking on it, ready to run and hide in the bushes at any moment. The need to concentrate constantly on possible sources of danger was exhausting, but they had to do it. In war you either paid attention, or you were dead.

Mahoney moved down the road with the help of the cane. He could have done without the cane, but it was a lot easier with it. It helped take some of his weight off his bad leg, and thereby diminished the pain. He thought the way he'd been wounded was strange. He and Cranepool had been in an exposed position, bullets were flying all around them, he got hit in the leg, and that fucking Cranepool didn't have a scratch on him. Somehow it didn't seem right. Moreover, Cranepool had fought at Salerno and Cassino and several other of the big battles in Italy, and had never been touched then either. Mahoney knew that the odds were starting to run against the kid. He was going to stop a bullet or a piece of shrapnel before long. Mahoney decided to stop thinking about that, because he liked Cranepool. Cranepool was a dopey kid, but he meant well. And he'd saved Mahoney's ass in Rouget.

"How're you feelin', Sarge?" Cranepool asked, walking beside him.

"Keep your eyes peeled."

"You been awful cranky today, Sarge."

"Shut up and stay alert."

Cranepool looked at the fields around him. This was flat farm country, not much different from Iowa, where he was from. He'd been raised on his father's hog farm along with three brothers and two sisters, and had been working on the farm since he was little. The work made him strong and the country air made him healthy. He'd often gone hunting with his father and his brothers, so he knew about guns and how to move silently through the woods. On the rifle range at Fort Leonard Wood, Missouri, he'd qualified as an expert with the M-1 and earned the highest score in his company. His company commander even had shaken his hand, but Cranepool wasn't surprised. He knew he was a crack shot.

"I hear something," Mahoney said.

Cranepool wrinkled his freckled nose. He wondered why Mahoney always heard things before he did.

"Off the road!" Mahoney ordered.

They dashed into the bushes, Mahoney taking huge hops with the aid of his cane. They got on their bellies and Mahoney looked through his binoculars. Far off in the distance he saw a little dot. It looked like a solitary automobile or truck, but as it came closer Mahoney could see that it was a motorcycle with a sidecar. He thought they'd just lie still and wait until it passed by, but then he remembered something.

"Hey, Cranepool," he said, "Didn't you tell me once that you used to own a motorcycle?"

"Sure—a Harley. It went like a son-of-a-bitch. I remember one time . . ."

Mahoney interrupted him. "Do you think you could drive a German motorcycle?"

Cranepool squinted and looked through the bushes. "Is that what's coming down the road?"

"Yeah, you ever take a good look at one?"

"Sure. They're very nice machines."

"You think you could drive one?"

"You don't say *drive* when you talk about motorcycles, Sarge. You say *ride.*"

"I'll say what the fuck I wanna say. I asked if you think you could drive one."

"I know I can. I had a chance to ride a couple of Germany Army motorcycles when I was in Italy. Like I said, they're very nice machines. They're much better than British motorcycles, but I don't think anybody ever has made a motorcycle as good as the Harley."

Mahoney spit into the ground. "Hey, Cranepool, I didn't ask for a fucking motorcycle lecture."

Leduc cleared his throat. He was a lean man of forty, with a mustache. "You are thinking maybe of capturing that motorcycle?"

"Yes," Mahoney replied. "If Cranepool can drive the fucking thing, maybe he can get both of us back to the American lines faster than we're going right now."

Leduc turned down the corners of his mouth. "That sounds like a good idea to me."

Mahoney looked through the binoculars and saw

the motorcycle more clearly now. One German was riding it and the other was sitting in the sidecar. Mahoney guessed that they were couriers of some kind. They might even have some important papers with them.

"Okay," Mahoney said, "when they come abreast of us, open fire and charge the bastards. Try not to do too much damage to the motorcycle. Any questions?"

Nobody said anything. Mahoney jammed a round into the chamber of his submachine gun and checked it out. He knew it was futile to have asked them not to damage the motorcycle, because they all were going to open fire and the bullets would go wherever they went. The main thing was to stop the motorcycle. They'd worry about the damage afterwards.

The motorcycle came roaring down the road, and the four men behind the bushes tensed with anticipation. They caught the rider and passenger in their sights and followed them as they came closer. Finally the motorcycle was directly in front of them, and Mahoney pulled the trigger of his submachine gun. It bucked and stuttered in his hands as a stream of bullets left its barrel and those of the submachine guns of Cranepool, Leduc, and Baudraye. The bullets descended like a rainfall of steel on the two German soldiers, ripping apart their uniforms and entering their bodies. The front wheel of the motorcycle wobbled and the rider leaned to the side, blood dripping from his nose and eyes. The motorcycle went off the road and into the gully on the far side, climbed up the gully, and became entangled in some bushes, its motor stalling and smoke issuing from its exhaust pipe.

"Up and at 'em!" Mahoney shouted.

The four of them charged through the bushes and onto the road, Mahoney leaving his cane behind. The motorcycle rider was lying in the gully and the passenger hung out the sidecar.

Mahoney looked at Leduc. "You and Baudraye strip off their uniforms."

"Yes, *Perroquet,*" said Leduc, using Mahoney's code name, the French word for parrot. Mahoney had acquired the name because of his ability to learn and mimic foreign languages quickly.

Mahoney turned to Cranepool. "See if you can get that motorcycle going."

Baudraye, a big burly Frenchman, pulled the German out of the sidecar and began removing his clothes. Leduc did the same thing with the German in the street, and Cranepool grabbed the handlebars of the motorcycle, tugging the vehicle backwards until it was free from the bushes. Mahoney leaned against a tree, his leg aching from the exertion, and watched Cranepool wheel the motorcycle into the gully and up to the road. The kid didn't look it, but he was strong as a mule.

"Wheels are okay, Sarge!" Cranepool called back.

Cranepool parked the motorcycle in the road and looked it over. There were dents and scratches but it seemed to be all right. He straddled it, turned the switch on, and kicked down the starter. Nothing happened.

"Uh-oh," Cranepool said.

"Get that fuckin' thing going!"

"I'm trying, Sarge."

Mahoney wished he had another cigar, but he was out of them. He took out a French cigarette and lit it with a match. Inhaling the harsh smoke, he looked down at his leg and could see blood seeping through the cloth of his pants. Fucking holes had opened up again. He thought they'd been hurting a little more than usual.

Leduc and Baudraye stood beside the motorcycle with the German uniforms over their arms and watched while Cranepool squatted beside the engine and snooped around. He found a broken sparkplug wire and spliced it together. The magneto had a bad dent in it but didn't appear to be damaged internally. The exhaust pipe was cracked, but that shouldn't make any big difference.

Cranepool mounted the motorcycle again and said a little prayer. He pumped the starter pedal a few times, then kicked it down. The motorcycle engine grumbled to life. Cranepool cheered and twisted the handlebar grip that also was the accelerator. The engine roared heartily. It was a BMW and could take a lot of punishment. Cranepool listened to it and realized that the timing was off a little, but not enough to matter. They only had to go about ten more miles.

"It's workin' Sarge!" he said happily.

Mahoney pushed himself away from the tree and limped toward the motorcycle. "Put on one of them uniforms!"

"Hup, Sarge."

Mahoney and Cranepool put on the German uniforms, which were much too small for both of them. Cranepool's arms extended several inches from the sleeves and he had no hope of pulling on the boots, but at least he could button up the tunic, which Mahoney couldn't.

Mahoney put the German helmet on his head and tied the strap under his chin. "I guess this will have to do," he said. "Let's get this show on the road."

Cranepool straddled the motorcycle that trembled with the beat of its engine. Mahoney turned to Leduc and Baudraye and shook their hands.

"Well, thanks for everything," he said.

"Good luck, *Perroquet.*"

"Good luck to the both of you. I hope that someday we can meet again."

"God willing we shall."

The two Frenchmen shook hands with Cranepool, and Mahoney got into the sidecar, sitting on the little seat. There wasn't much room in there for a man his size, and he had to bring his heels close to his fanny, which made his leg ache more. He and Cranepool pulled the goggles down over their eyes.

The Frenchmen stepped back and Cranepool dropped it into first. He let out the clutch, twisted the accelerator, and the motorcycle moved forward. It gathered speed and Cranepool shifted into second. The motorcycle zoomed down the road, the sidecar jouncing around, and Mahoney held his submachine gun tightly in his hands, hoping there wouldn't be much trouble ahead, because he wasn't feeling too well. He'd lost a lot of blood during the past few days and had become weak and woozy.

"How're you doin', Sarge!" Cranepool yelled over his shoulder.

"Keep your fuckin' eyes on the road!"

"Hup, Sarge!"

The wind whipped Mahoney's face, and the countryside whizzed past his eyes. The bouncing of the sidecar made his stomach queasy and he thought he might vomit his lunch. I hate this fucking war, he thought.

It wasn't long before they approached the convoy of eight personnel carriers that they'd seen a short while ago. Cranepool steered to the right and passed them slowly, because his rate of speed wasn't much faster than theirs. The wheels of the trucks threw back mud and gunk that splattered onto Cranepool's and Mahoney's uniforms. Mahoney looked into the rear of the trucks. The German soldiers were still hunched over, trying to grab some sleep.

Cranepool passed the convoy and charged forward on the open road. It was three o'clock in the afternoon and the sound of battle was coming closer. In the distance he could see the town of Carentan. He figured they should get there in about a half-hour, and then the fun would begin.

Mahoney bent low in the sidecar and lit another cigarette. Like Cranepool, he knew they'd be in the thick of the front line fighting in just a little while, and he didn't look forward to it very much because his leg hurt and he felt dizzy. He didn't feel up to a fight just then, and he knew how dangerous it was to be that way. A combat soldier has to be at peak efficiency at all times, and once he loses that fine-honed edge, he becomes a candidate for the cemetery. He gritted his teeth and tried to convince himself that he wasn't as badly off as he truly was. He shook his shoulders and growled.

Cranepool glanced back. "You all right, Sarge?"

"Keep your fucking eyes on the road!"

"We're gonna be in Carentan pretty soon!"

"Don't stop for anything!"

"Hup, Sarge!

They passed a company of German soldiers walking in a column of twos toward Carentan, and the Germans were dragging ass. Mahoney figured they'd been on the march for a long time and if they went right up on the line they wouldn't last long, unless the American soldiers were dragging ass too.

Mahoney closed his eyes to slits and the town of Carentan blurred in the distance. In his dazed and comatose state, he thought of how nice it would be if he could take a hot shower and then go to sleep in a clean bed. When he woke up he'd have a steak and a bottle of beer, and then he'd go out and find himself a frisky young girl. Mahoney hadn't had any sex for a while and wanted very much to crawl into the sack with a frisky young girl, the kind that scratched and bit you and did all sorts of weird things. At various times, depending on his moods, Mahoney craved tall girls, short girls, fat girls, skinny girls, crazy girls, smart girls, young girls or old girls, but right now he had a taste for a young one who was utterly depraved.

"We're comin' into town, Sarge!"

Mahoney opened his eyes and saw the town coming up fast, only it didn't look like the Carentan he'd seen a few months ago. That town had been clean and solid, whereas this town was nearly destroyed by bombs and artillery shells. The din of battle was quite close; he could smell gunpowder and corpses. Evidently the fighting was taking place on the far side of the town, a few miles down the road.

Cranepool slowed down and the motorcycle sputtered through the town, passing columns of soldiers moving toward or coming back from the front. Cranepool threaded the motorcycle skillfully among them and the hospital trucks and *kubelwagens*. Many buildings only had one wall standing, and they passed one undamaged building that was being used as a field hospital. Mahoney saw a couple of nurses in front and wondered if they were frisky young girls.

"Uh-oh," said Cranepool.

Mahoney looked ahead and saw that they were approaching an intersection in whose center stood an SS man in black uniform and helmet, signaling for them to halt.

"Should I stop, Sarge?"

"Yeah, and let me do the talking. If I tell you *move out,* that means *move out,* you got me?"

"I gotcha, Sarge."

Cranepool braked the motorcycle and it glided to a stop in front of the SS man, whose left collar patch indicated that his rank was equivalent to that of a staff sergeant in the U.S. Army.

"Let me see your papers," said the SS man, holding out his hand. He had deep-set spooky eyes and needed a shave.

Mahoney stood up in the sidecar and looked at the SS man, who was directly in front of him. "I'm sorry, but I don't have time," Mahoney said in perfect German.

The SS man blinked, but his tone of voice and expression didn't change. "I said let me see your papers."

"Get out of my way, I don't have time."

"Don't have time?" the SS man asked. "I think perhaps a few months in the stockade might make you wish you took the time."

"Move out!" Mahoney screamed, dropping into the sidecar.

Cranepool let the clutch lever loose and twisted the accelerator as far as it would go. The engine stalled. The SS man took a step backwards and reached for his service revolver, but Mahoney brought his submachine gun up fast and opened fire before the German could aim. Mahoney's first bullets slammed into the mud but the next ones caught the German on the kneecap, and as Mahoney raised the jerking, twisting submachine gun the SS man's body was torn apart. He stumbled backwards, dead on his feet, as Cranepool frantically jumped up and down on the starter. The engine came alive again, sputtering and farting. Cranepool let the clutch lever loose more smoothly this time, and didn't twist the accelerator so far. The rear wheel spun out on the mud, and the motorcycle darted forward. German soldiers nearby ran into the street to look at the SS man, as Cranepool skidded around the first corner.

Mahoney hung onto the rim of the sidecar. "You fuckin' asshole!" he yelled.

"I didn't do nothing, Sarge!" Cranepool replied as he dodged a donkey standing dumbly in the middle of the street.

"You stalled the motorcycle!"

"I couldn't help it!"

"Asshole!"

"How was I supposed to know you were gonna shoot the bastard?"

"Did you think I was gonna whistle Dixie with him?"

"How should I know?"

"You'd better know how to get us out of here, you little fuck!"

"Leave it to me, Sarge!"

Cranepool turned the next corner and realized he didn't know where he was. He decided that his best bet would be to head for the sound of the fighting, because that's where the Americans were. He zoomed past a row of one and two-story houses that hadn't been damaged too badly by shelling and bombing, turned left, and accelerated toward the front lines.

Mahoney fed a fresh clip of ammunition into his submachine gun, his teeth chattering. That one had been a little too close for comfort. He didn't feel up to shit like that with his leg bleeding and his head spinning. Something told him he wasn't going to get out of this one alive. They were going to shoot him like a dog in the middle of the road and that would be the end of him. Oh what a fucking miserable war.

Cranepool was on the road leading out of town, zipping along at sixty miles an hour. He passed a column of German Tiger tanks heading for the front, and then heard the ominous sound of aircraft overhead. He looked up and out of the clouds came diving a swarm of American fighter planes.

"Get off the road, you asshole!" Mahoney yelled.

Cranepool lurched to the right and went down a gully on the side of the road. He accelerated up the incline and the motorcycle flew into the air, giving Mahoney a queasy feeling in his stomach. The motorcycle landed on its rear wheel first and Cranepool poured on the coal. The tiny vehicle flew across a field, as the fighters strafed the road behind them. Mahoney looked back and could see tankers battening down their hatches and German troops running in all directions. One of the fighters shot its cannon at a Tiger tank and blew it to smithereens. Another fighter scored a direct hit on another tank, and a third one missed its target, blowing a huge hole in the road instead.

Ahead was a stone wall about four feet high. Cranepool steered to the right, found an opening in it, and barreled through. He stormed up a hill and down the other side. Hitting a bump, the motorcycle soared into the air, and slowly came down.

"Cut that shit out!" Mahoney screamed.

"Hup, Sarge!"

Hup Sarge your ass, Mahoney thought, bouncing up and down in the sidecar. He looked back at the road and was pleased to see that the American fighter planes were decimating the German column. An artillery shell whistled through the sky and fell to earth fifty yards away, blowing mud and stones into the air, and some fell on Mahoney and Cranepool. Ahead was a forest that extended from left to right as far as the eye could see. Smoke trailed into the sky from various points in the forest, and a huge orange ball of flame exploded on Mahoney's left.

"Hey, Sarge, I just thought of something!" Cranepool called over his shoulder. "When our guys see us they're gonna think we're Germans and they're gonna shoot at us!"

"Let me worry about that!" Mahoney replied.

"What're you gonna do?"

"Just keep driving and leave everything else to me!"

"Hup, Sarge!"

Cranepool twisted the accelerator and shifted up. The motorcycle sped across the field, passing shell craters and dead Germans. Mahoney reached into his back pocket and took out a dirty handkerchief. It wasn't very big and it wasn't very white, but if he waved it in the air maybe the Americans wouldn't shoot.

Cranepool shifted down and decelerated as the motorcycle entered the woods. He steered among the trees and thought that the Germans might consider it odd for their motorcycle couriers to be riding in the woods instead of the road. He wondered if someone in Carentan had sent a report forward that there was a renegade motorcycle courier on the loose. If so, trouble could be expected.

They came to a section of the forest that had been blown up. Two dead Germans were lying face down in the mud, and Mahoney noticed hand grenades affixed to their belts.

"Stop the motorcycle!" Mahoney shouted.

"What for?"

"Because I said so!"

Cranepool braked and shifted down. "What's the matter?"

"Get me those hand grenades over there."

Cranepool dismounted and ran toward the dead Germans. They were starting to stink so he held his breath and took the hand grenades off their belts. There were five in all, and he brought them back to Mahoney, dumping them into his lap.

"Here you go, Sarge."

"Get on that motorcycle and move out."

"Hup, Sarge."

Cranepool mounted up and they drove off again. The sound of battle was quite close now, and Mahoney figured they'd be in the thick of it pretty soon. He had his white handkerchief ready between his legs and his submachine gun in his hands.

Ahead, Cranepool saw a row of German trenches. "Hey, Sarge, should I go over them?"

"Well, you sure as hell can't go under them!"

Cranepool shifted down and wound out the accelerator. The motorcycle bucked forward and raced toward the trenches. The Germans in the trenches looked behind them and were astonished to see the motorcycle and sidecar approaching at top speed. They ducked their heads, and Cranepool pulled back on his handlebars. The motorcycle sailed into the air and spewed exhaust smoke into the trench. It landed, Cranepool dodged a tree, then a rock, and accelerated again. He steered around another trench and the Germans in it cheered them on, thinking he and Mahoney were on their side.

A shell exploded nearby, knocking down some trees. The brush was getting thick. Bullets whizzed through the air, and Cranepool thought they might be in no-man's-land.

"Try to get back on the road," Mahoney said.

"I don't know where the fuck the road is!"

Mahoney pointed to his right. "It's over there."

"I think we should keep going straight, Sarge. Somebody's liable to stop us on the road."

"Okay, go straight! Just get the fuck moving!"

"Hup, Sarge!"

Cranepool threaded through the trees, and Mahoney was having serious doubts that they were going to make it through. They passed more trenches, some of them firing mortars into the air. The rattle of machine-gun fire came from up ahead, and another shell exploded harmlessly nearby. Things were getting a little hot in the woods. He realized that the enemy's defense was in considerable depth, deployed that way to absorb attacks. Sooner or later, probably sooner, he and Cranepool would come to the front of the German defenses, and then the shit really would hit the fan.

"Hey, what are you doing out here!" called a German soldier in a trench.

"The same thing you're doing out here!" Mahoney replied.

Twenty yards later a German officer sitting in a trench asked if they were lost.

"No," replied Mahoney, "we know where we're going, sir!"

"We do?" asked Cranepool.

"Shaddup!"

They continued to make their way through the woods, passing Germans in trenches and artillery emplacements firing shells at the American lines. The deployment became gradually thicker as they moved along, and then Mahoney saw light through the trees. Cranepool saw it, too, as he steered around obstacles and moved steadily forward. It was the battlefield.

"Stop here!" Mahoney said.

Cranepool braked, and when the motorcycle stopped he stood up and looked through his binoculars. Through the prismatic tubes he saw the edge of the forest straight ahead, and beyond it was a grassy field that inclined downwards toward a little river, and then upwards toward another forest where the Americans evidently were. The other forest was approximately 800 yards away, too far for small arms fire to be effective but a good staging area for an attack. It was inevitable that sooner or later either the Germans or the Americans would mount one against each other. Puffs of smoke and explosions could be seen in the forest where the Americans were.

Mahoney pointed ahead. "That's where we've got to go."

"I'm ready when you are."

"Just hang on a minute."

Mahoney looked through the binoculars, trying to find a clear section where they could break through without getting too many machine-gun bullets in their backs. He saw a long trench that appeared to be filled with only riflemen, and at the end of the trench was an artillery emplacement featuring one 88, the piece the Germans used against both aircraft and tanks. Mahoney doubted whether that 88 could be aimed quickly enough to hit a fast-moving motorcycle.

Mahoney pointed in the direction he wanted Cranepool to go. "You see that trench over there?"

"Over where?"

Mahoney handed him the binoculars and pointed again. "Over there."

Cranepool looked through the binoculars. "You mean the long trench with the 88 on the end?"

"Yeah. I want you to go right over it the way you went over those trenches we passed, and then I want you to head for the American lines as fast as you can."

Cranepool looked at the field and the river at its bottom. "Hope that river isn't too deep."

"If it's too deep, we'll abandon the motorcycle and swim the fucking thing."

"We'll be sitting ducks for the riflemen up here."

"They won't be able to hit us."

"But we won't be that far away, Sarge."

"We'll be moving too fast for them to draw a bead on us. What's the matter with you, Cranepool, are you scared or something?"

"Scared? Me? No, I'm not scared, Sarge." He lowered the binoculars and turned around. "I just thought I'd raise certain military considerations."

"Stop trying to talk like an officer, you fucking asshole. Get going and keep your head down. Once we get in that field there, take every evasive action you know."

"Hup, Sarge."

Cranepool blipped the engine, and Mahoney pulled the pin on two of the German hand grenades. If he was going to die, he intended to leave this earth in a big blast. Cranepool shifted into first and twisted the accelerator. The motorcycle moved forward and Cranepool steered it around trees and bushes, making slow but steady progress toward the trench Mahoney had told him to jump over. He maneuvered the motorcycle until he had a clear path to the trench ahead, and the German soldiers in other trenches looked at him curiously.

"Where are you going with that thing?" one of the soldiers asked jokingly.

"Up your ass," Cranepool mumbled as he accelerated away.

Mahoney gritted his teeth and held on tightly as the motorcycle gathered speed. The trench came up fast and he thought okay this is it. Cranepool pulled back on the handlebars and the motorcycle was in the air, directly over the trench. Mahoney dropped one of the hand grenades into the Germans below, then twisted and flung the other at the 88 emplacement. The motorcycle landed on the ground and Cranepool wound it out. It streaked down the hill at a slight angle to the river below, and suddenly Cranepool changed direction and went the other way. Mahoney looked back and saw the hand grenades explode one after the other. Arms, legs, and heads flew up out of the trench but only a puff of smoke and a fireball issued from the 88 emplacement. Mahoney figured the Germans inside were splattered against the walls of the fortifications they'd made, but that was tough shit for them.

He'd heard machine guns and rifles firing during the time they'd been in the woods, but now the bullets whistled over his head and he realized the

Germans had got wise and were firing at them. The sidecar bounced around so much he couldn't return the fire effectively, so he ducked his head and prayed that God would help him escape, although he was a terrible sinner and a lapsed Catholic, he hadn't been to Mass for years, and back when he'd been married he'd committed adultery so many times it wasn't even funny.

Cranepool zig-zagged down the hill, remembering all the motorcycle races he'd run on his good old Harley, and how similar this was, except that now he was trying to outrace bullets in an effort to save his skin. Bullets whapped into the ground all around him and whistled past his ears. He knew that the Americans in the forest ahead could see what was happening, and he wondered what they were thinking. Finally he neared the bottom of the hill and the river loomed ahead.

"Should I stop?" he asked over his shoulder.

"Are you crazy? Keep going. you stupid asshole!"

"But what if it's too deep?"

"It's not too deep! Just go right through it!"

Whether it was deep or not, Cranepool knew that the water would slow the motorcycle down and maybe stop it. The only thing to do was give it all the gas he could and barrel right through. He shifted down and twisted the accelerator as far as it would go. The rear wheel bit into the mud and the motorcycle leapt forward. Mahoney saw the river approach and held onto the sidecar so that he wouldn't get knocked out when they hit the water. It was only fifteen yards wide and didn't appear to be very deep. They'd just slosh through it and climb the hill to safety. He'd be in a nice warm bed within an hour, maybe with frisky young nurses playing with his joint.

The motorcycle splashed into the water and in two seconds Cranepool was in up to his shoulders. The water was over Mahoney's head, and he struggled to get out of the sidecar as he gurgled and sputtered. The river had been deeper than he'd thought. He kicked with his feet, felt a violent ache in his left leg, and cleared the sidecar, his head breaking the surface of the fast-moving river.

"You okay, Sarge?" Cranepool asked, treading water.

"Yeah, you?"

"Yeah. I thought you said the river wasn't very deep."

"Fuck you, Cranepool."

"What now, Sarge?"

"We've got to make it up the hill, Cranepool. Move fast and make a low silhouette."

They swam across the river as its current dragged them downstream and bullets splashed around them. Every time Mahoney kicked his left leg he thought the damn thing would fall off, but he kept going because not to do so would be to die. His arms were strong and gradually he pulled himself to the far shore, although Cranepool got there first and pulled him out of the water.

"How're you feeling, Sarge?"

"Get moving, Cranepool!"

They ran up the hill in a zig-zag fashion, keeping their heads down. Mahoney limped badly and his head was spinning. Glancing at his leg, he saw blood oozing through his pants. Bullets zapped into the gound near them and halfway up the hill they heard a shell coming in. Dropping to their stomachs, they heard the shell explode ahead of them, and then they were on their feet again, running through the smoke and muck toward the top of the hill.

Mahoney began to doubt whether he'd make it. He was giving orders to his left leg but it wasn't responding very well. God, if you get me out of this one I'll go to Mass every Sunday and say a Rosary every night. He felt like lying down on the ground and giving up, and knew that was the time you had to push the hardest. Then he heard a barrage of gunfire coming from the American lines. They were firing cannon, howitzers, machine guns—everything they had—and Mahoney realized that they were trying to cover him and Cranepool. Almost simultaneously, German bullets stopped buzzing around him and Cranepool. American firepower was pinning the Germans down.

That gave Mahoney encouragement. He looked up the hill and saw that there was only fifty yards to go. He gasped and clawed the ground, struggling to make it to the American lines. Cranepool reached back with his long arm, grabbed Mahoney's jacket, and pulled him along. Mahoney reached into his back pocket and took out his white handkerchief, waving it in the air.

"We're American soldiers!" he screamed. "Don't shoot!"

He tripped over a rock and fell on his chin. Cranepool yanked him to his feet and up the hill he went again. Bullets and artillery shells streaked over their heads on their way to the German positions. The American trenches came closer and Mahoney could see the GIs peering over the battlements.

"Don't shoot, we're Americans!"

A squad of the GIs came out of the trenches and ran down the hill to help Mahoney and Cranepool. They grabbed their arms and dragged them the remaining few yards into the trenches. and they all dove in together.

Mahoney was at the bottom of the heap and his leg was killing him, but he was safe. For the first time in three months he was behind his own lines, and it felt good to be back. He wanted to shout for joy, but that would be undignified for a master sergeant in the United States Army, so he just kept his mouth shut and waited patiently for the American soldiers to pile off him.

TWO

"What have we got here!" asked a florid-faced captain, sitting behind a folding desk in a command post tent in the forest.

"They claim to be American soldiers, sir," said the buck sergeant in charge of the squad that had brought Cranepool and Mahoney to the captain.

To the left of the captain stood a tall, gawky lieutenant wearing glasses. "Be careful, sir. They might be spies."

"We already took away their weapons, sir," the buck sergeant said, displaying two commando knives, a Luger, a Walther PPK, and two German hand grenades. He also showed the captured dispatch pouch.

The captain frowned as he rose from behind his desk. It was raining again and a pitter-patter could be heard on the roof of the tent. The captain placed his hands behind his back and walked toward Mahoney and Cranepool, who were standing at attention. The captain was short, with a barrel chest and bandy legs.

Cranepool cleared his throat. "I don't want to speak out of turn, sir, or anything like that, but could you get a doctor for Sergeant Mahoney here?"

"I'll ask the questions," the captain said, looking at Mahoney's leg, the pants of which were soaked with blood. "Who are you birds anyway?"

Mahoney cleared his throat. "Master Sergeant Clarence J. Mahoney, Twenty-Third Rangers, R.A. one-one-two-eight-two-two-oh-three," he said.

"Corporal Edward Cranepool, also Twenty-Third Rangers, R.A. five-six-one-three-three-one-nine-five."

The lieutenant wearing the eyeglasses wrote the information down. The inside of the tent smelled like new canvas. Mahoney thought he was going to faint at any moment.

The captain stood in front of Mahoney. "What in the fuck are you doing in those German uniforms?"

"We were dropped behind German lines around three months ago," Mahoney said, "and we've been working with the Free French. Yesterday we were ordered to return to our own lines, and on our way back we picked up the uniforms."

The lieutenant sniffed the air suspiciously. "Be careful, sir. They might be lying."

"If you'll contact the Twenty-Third Rangers, sir," Mahoney said, "I'm sure they'll verify what I told you." He was struggling to maintain his consciousness, but suddenly his eyes filled with black ink and he dropped to the floor.

Cranepool looked down at him. "He's been shot in the leg, sir."

The captain looked at the buck sergeant. "Get some medics in here."

"Yes, sir." The buck sergeant ran out of the tent.

The lieutenant cleared his throat. "This might be a trick, sir."

"Oh, shut up," the captain replied wearily.

The lieutenant looked hurt, and bit his lower lip. The buck sergeant returned with two medics who dived on Mahoney. They cut open his pants and looked at the ugly purple wound. Putting a sulfa dressing on it, they gave him a shot of morphine, then stood up.

"He needs to be evacuated to a hospital," one of the medics said to the captain.

The captain looked at the medic. "Take him to the hospital." He looked at the buck sergeant. "You go with them and stand guard over him until we find out who he really is."

"He's really Sergeant Mahoney," Cranepool said hopefully.

"Speak when you're spoken to, soldier," the captain replied gruffly.

"Sorry, sir."

The medics rolled Mahoney onto a stretcher and carried him out of the tent. Cranepool watched him go, wondering when he'd see his old sergeant again.

The lieutenant stepped forward. "May I question him, sir?" he asked, referring to Cranepool.

"What the fuck for?"

"He might have important and valuable information, sir."

"You wouldn't know what to do with it if he did. Call Battalion Intelligence and tell somebody there to track down the Twenty-Third Rangers, and see if these two birds are part of them."

"Yes, sir."

The lieutenant moved to the field telephone, and the captain looked at Cranepool again. "When'd you eat last?"

"Sometime yesterday, sir," Cranepool lied.

The captain looked at a corporal who was among the squad that had escorted Mahoney and Cranepool into the tent. "Take him to the mess tent for some chow, and then keep an eye on him."

"Yes, sir."

"May I ask a question, sir?" Cranepool said.

"What is it?"

"Can I take this German uniform off, sir?"

"Yes, but don't do it here. I don't want the damned thing."

"Thank you, sir."

"Get out of here, all of you."

They all saluted. "Yes, sir!"

They did an about-face and marched Cranepool out of the tent.

THREE

The battalion intelligence office contacted the Twenty-Third Rangers and learned that Mahoney and Cranepool were indeed part of that unit. After receiving treatment for his wounded leg, Mahoney was evacuated by truck to the nearest airfield and flown to England, where he became a patient at the big U.S. Army hospital in Southwick, a suburb of London.

Cranepool stayed overnight in the company that had rescued him, and the next day orders came down assigning him to Headquarters Company of the Twenty-Third Rangers, which was killing Germans somewhere on the Cherbourg Peninsula. He was put in a jeep and driven back to the big replacement depot near the town of La Madeleine, where he was supposed to await transportation to the Twenty-Third Rangers.

He arrived at the replacement company at 1400 hours, long after chow had been served, and he was hungry again. He reported to a first lieutenant nearly as young as he who told him to draw a uniform at the quartermaster's, and then sit tight and listen for his name to be called on the bitch box.

Cranepool went to the quartermaster's, which was a big prefabricated building that didn't look as though it'd survive the next puff of wind that came by. Inside, he gave the chit to the sergeant and drew brown pants, khaki shirt, combat boots, cartridge belt, helmet, and poncho. He put these on and looked at himself in a mirror, pleased to be in uniform again after so many months in civilian clothes. He knew that he looked good in a uniform and generally made a good impression on officers. He figured he would make a splendid officer someday.

He went to the latrine, where he found a lively crap game in progress. Throughout his military career, whenever he'd gone to a latrine, there usually had been a crap game in progress. This was because the lights in latrines were kept on all night, thereby affording nonstop visibility for crap games that continued for days and even weeks, with participants constantly coming and going.

He watched the crap game for a while, wishing he had some money to bet, but he wouldn't be paid until he got to the Twenty-Third Rangers, and he doubted whether disbursements were being made on the front lines. He figured that the Army owed him a few hundred dollars in back pay.

It was raining outside, but he didn't feel like hanging around the latrine any longer. He went outside to get some fresh air and maybe bum a cigarette from somebody. In front of the latrine was a large parade ground surrounded by rows of pup tents, wall tents, prefabricated buildings, and water towers. *"Private Collins, report to the Orderly Room!"* said the bitch box on top of a nearby pole.

Cranepool put his hands in his pockets and walked

onto the parade ground. Rain fell moderately heavy, but his poncho kept him dry and the air smelled clean and fresh. He thought about Sergeant Mahoney and wondered what he was doing right now. Cranepool missed Mahoney; they'd been together nearly every day during the three months they'd been in France. He thought Mahoney was the greatest, toughest soldier he'd ever seen, and although Cranepool only was twenty years old, he'd seen a lot of tough ones in Italy. He hoped he'd run into Mahoney again someday, but knew that he might not. Reassignments sometimes were crazy in the Army. You never knew where you'd wind up. At least he was going back to his old outfit, the Twenty-Third Rangers.

Six big trucks drove onto the middle of the parade ground area, and men spilled out of tents and buildings, running like mad toward the trucks. Cranepool had no idea what was going on, but figured it must be something good, so he broke into a trot and joined the rush. He came to a big crowd of soldiers and asked one of them what was going on.

"Coffee and donuts from the Red Cross," the soldier said.

Cranepool's heart soared with happiness. He'd been hungry, and now they were going to serve donuts, which were one of his favorite foods. He got in one of the lines leading to the trucks, which were being unloaded by Red Cross people and military personnel. Cranepool hoped the Red Cross was giving out cigarettes with the coffee and donuts.

Two big wall tents were pitched, and the lines

readjusted so that they led to the openings of the tents. Cranepool licked his lips in anticipation of the donuts. Although they had coffee in France, he'd never seen a donut. This would be his first donut in months, and he was literally drooling.

Then he noticed a curious thing. The line that he was in was much longer than the other line. He didn't know why, and at first thought he should stay in the line he was in, and not worry about it, but he couldn't help thinking that if he got into the other line he could get his coffee and donuts quicker. He closed his eyes and imagined that he could smell the steaming coffee and fresh donuts. The Red Cross was a great organization—no question about it.

He opened his eyes again and looked at the shorter line. Why weren't the other guys going over there? Well, if they were going to be assholes about it, he wasn't. He was a clever fellow and probably would become an officer before long. He knew that officers had to take the initiative and do bold things. So he simply put his hands into his pockets, whistled a little tune, and left the line he was in, walking casually to the shorter line, where he took his position behind a nervous little soldier whose helmet was crooked on his head.

Although this line was about half the size of the other line, it still was a very long line. Perhaps two hundred soldiers were in front of him, and Cranepool shuffled ahead inch by inch, permitting himself to daydream, but not to the extent where he wouldn't know if his name was called over the bitch box. He hoped his name wouldn't be called before he got his coffee and donut, and if he was lucky, they might even give him *two* donuts.

Slowly the line moved forward. The soldiers around him were joking and carrying on, but some sergeants were in line and nobody dared get too rowdy. Cranepool was happy to be back with American troops. It was safe and secure here, without too much to worry about, whereas behind enemy lines there had been constant anxiety about the Gestapo and French collaborators who might inform on him. When you were behind enemy lines you never knew who you could trust, and that could make you crazy after a while.

The line steadily moved forward and Cranepool drew closer to the tent. He noticed it didn't have a chimney on top of it like the other tent, and figured that maybe they were making the coffee in the other tent and bringing some to this second tent. Perhaps that's why the line to the other tent was longer: because the troops thought the coffee would be hotter there, but Cranepool didn't give a damn about the coffee, he just wanted donuts and cigarettes.

Finally he approached the front of the tent. He saw that a sergeant was standing there, letting the soldiers in one at a time. He wondered why they were doing that? Maybe the soldiers had been causing too much commotion around the coffee and donuts, stealing extra food and maybe pinching the women, if there were any women around.

Cranepool came to the head of the line and the sergeant looked at him as though he was a piece of shit. The sergeant had a chin like a gorilla and it was covered with a five o'clock shadow although it was only two-thirty in the afternoon. A shiver went up

Cranepool's back, and he wondered why all the old sergeants were so damned nasty. It was as though all of them took nasty pills.

Somebody inside the tent said *next,* and the sergeant told Cranepool to go inside. Cranepool stepped between the tent flaps and saw three old sergeants at a table that had a crate on it and two crates beside it. Cranepool wondered where the coffee urn and donuts were. Four canvas stalls were at the far end of the tent, and a soldier slouched out of one of them, heading for the flap at the rear of the tent.

"Next!" said a grizzled old sergeant at the table.

Cranepool walked up to him. "Where's the coffee and donuts, Sarge?"

The sergeant blinked. "Coffee and donuts! Why you fucking birdbrain, this is the Pro Station!"

"Pro Station?" Cranepool asked weakly.

"Yeah. Here's your kit. Take it back to one of the stalls back there and use it."

In the dimness of the tent, the sergeant pushed a little cardboard box across the table to Cranepool.

Cranepool smiled. "I made a mistake, Sarge. I got in the wrong line by mistake."

"Bullshit!" the sergeant exploded. "You take that Pro Kit to one of the stalls back there and use it, you hear me?"

"Hup, Sarge," Cranepool said, picking up the Pro Kit.

"I want you to bring the empty tube back to me to make sure, and don't be cute and try to hide the shit someplace, because I'll have your ass. You got me, young soldier?"

"I got you, Sarge."

"Get moving!"

"Hup, Sarge."

His heart sinking, thinking about the coffee and donuts he was missing because he foolishly had got into the wrong line, Cranepool walked back to the open canvas stall, pulled the canvas shut, and stood in the darkness, taking the wrapper off the Pro Kit. In the next stall a guy was grunting and farting. Cranepool cursed himself for coming to this tent. He should have asked somebody. Pro Stations were for guys who'd got laid recently and thought they might have venereal disease. Pro Kits were supposed to stop venereal disease provided you used them right after you got laid.

Cranepool took the little khaki tube out of the box and held it up to his eyes. On its end was a nozzle that you were supposed to insert into the hole in your dick, and then squeeze the contents of the tube into your dick. The medicine was supposed to kill the venereal disease germs, if you had any. Cranepool didn't think he had any, but he wasn't sure. A few days ago he'd screwed a French woman named Louise, and although she was a very nice person from a good family, he knew that she screwed around a lot, and who could tell what kind of filthy bastards she might have been screwing? For all Cranepool knew, she might have had a terrible venereal disease, and you never could tell about women because it didn't show on them the way it did on men.

Cranepool broke out into a cold sweat as he remembered the venereal disease movie they'd shown him at Fort Benning, Georgia, before he shipped out for Italy. The movie had depicted guys with their dicks literally rotting off from venereal disease. The dicks had been green and filled with every kind of pus imaginable. The narrator of the movie said that guys sometimes went crazy and even died from venereal disease. Then the movie showed how they tried to cure venereal disease. They stuck a big long needle into a man's dick, and then turned a knob that made the tip of the needle into a little clawlike apparatus. Then they dragged this claw right up the man's dick, bringing blood, pus, and infected flesh along with it, and Cranepool had nearly fainted in the movie theatre. Guys were puking into their handerchiefs and sergeants strolled around punching guys who closed their eyes because they couldn't bear to look any longer. After it was over, Cranepool swore that he'd never screw again in his life, but of course, like all the other GIs, he did not keep this promise very long.

And now, in the little canvas stall, he thought of the movie with its rotting dicks and needles and little claws on the end. He remembered Louise and wondered if she'd given him a dose. Maybe she had. Maybe his dick was going to start rotting away. You were supposed to use the Pro Kit right after you got laid, and that had been several days ago, but maybe it would still work. He'd watch his dick very carefully for the next few weeks, making sure that no scabs or cankers appeared on the head. He hoped the venereal disease didn't make him crazier than he was already.

Unbuttoning his fly, he took out his sorrowful little dick and let it hang in the humid atmosphere of the tent. Then he tore the end off the tube, grabbed his dick with his left hand, and inserted the end of the tube into the little eye on its head. He squeezed the tube, and felt the stuff enter his dick. A weird sensation ensued, as though the stuff was flowing into his balls and even into the heels of his feet. When the tube was empty he withdrew it, put his dick back where it belonged, and buttoned up his pants. He left the stall and carried the empty tube to the sergeant at the desk, who was pushing a Pro Kit toward another GI.

"Here you go, Sarge," Cranepool said, holding the empty tube in the palm of his hand.

The sergeant squinted at it. "In the bucket, shitface."

Cranepool dropped the tube into the bucket. "Can I go now, Sarge?"

"Get the fuck out of here before I make you take another one," the sergeant growled.

Cranepool ran out of the tent and looked around to see if the other tent was still serving coffee and donuts. There was a line in front of it, and Cranepool thought that maybe the afternoon wouldn't be a total loss after all. He trotted through the rain toward the end of the line, his poncho flapping around his long legs, and took his place at its end. The tent in front of him had a chimney sticking out the top, but Cranepool decided he shouldn't take any more chances. He tapped the shoulder of the guy in front of him, and the guy turned around. He had a big red nose and his eyes were half-closed.

"Whatcha want?" the guy asked in an unfriendly manner.

"Is this the coffee and donuts tent?" Cranepool asked.

"Of course it's the coffee and donut tent. What are you, dumb or something?"

Cranepool shrugged. "Just thought I'd make sure," he said.

FOUR

It was night at SHAEF Headquarters in Bushy Park near London, and General Dwight D. Eisenhower, the Supreme Commander, was alone in his office poring over his maps. A solitary lamp overhead directed light onto the map, and the rest of the room was shrouded in darkness.

Ike looked down at the city of Caen on the Orne River. The British Second Army under the command of General Bernard Law Montgomery was supposed to have taken the city immediately after landing on the Normandy beaches, but it was the 12th of June and he still hadn't done so. The city was important because it controlled the road net that lead to the heart of France. Whoever controlled Caen controlled troop movements between the coast and Central France and Monty's forces had to take it soon, yet it didn't appear as though they'd take it in the near future.

The problem was that the Germans also knew of Caen's significance, and had rushed the Twenty-First Panzer Division there upon learning of the Allied landings in the vicinity. Since then the Germans had transferred divisions from other parts of France to Caen, sending them into attack as soon as they were brought up on the line.

Monty's forces had been taking a terrific pounding, and it was no wonder that he couldn't move forward. Yet it was a miracle that he hadn't been pushed backwards. And surprisingly, the situation at Caen might prove to be beneficial, because Monty was destroying the German divisions one by one as soon as they attacked.

Ike thought the Germans might get better results if they marshalled their forces and attacked en masse. They might be able to push Monty into the sea, and there was the ever-present danger that they might do it yet. Yet Monty said he didn't think they would. He'd fought Rommel before in Africa and knew his style. Rommel attacked as soon as he could with whatever he had. He believed in always keeping his enemy off balance, and never giving him a chance to mount an offensive, but Monty was ready for Rommel and knew how to handle him. He'd certainly been handling him all right so far, slowly chewing up his forces.

Monty could be expected to wear down Rommel's forces, provided Ike could keep Monty supplied with fresh troops, tanks, ammunition, and gas. Otherwise Monty and the rest of the invasion force could very well be pushed into the sea.

The key to the issue at Caen was the supply situation. An army might be in a perfect position to attack, but could not do so if it lacked the wherewithal to wage war. Ike was facing great difficulties in his efforts to supply his invasion force. He had no natural port, so artificial ports had been constructed on the beaches of Normandy, but they were nowhere as efficient as a natural port, and a hurricane a few days ago had nearly destroyed most of the artificial port area.

Therefore it was important that he secure a real port at once. The Normandy area had been selected as the invasion site on D-Day because, among other reasons, it was close to the huge port of Cherbourg. Ike believed that it was imperative for the American forces which were closest to Cherbourg to capture the port as soon as possible. If he had the port he could easily resupply his beachhead and insure that Monty could hold Caen. If the port could not be taken, the invasion might fail, and if the invasion failed, the war would be lost.

Ike decided that the time had come to make a major all-out push on the port of Cherbourg. The future of the war may very well hang in the balance over it. If he could take Cherbourg soon, he was certain he could hold the beachhead forever, and then Monty could move north and capture the port of Antwerp. With Cherbourg and Antwerp, and the help of the Allied forces, Ike's ground troops could move resolutely across Europe to Berlin, and maybe win the war by the end of the year.

Ike bent closer to the map and looked at the little flags and pins. He saw that the VII Corps, commanded by General "Lightning Joe" Collins, was closest to the Cherbourg Peninsula. Lightning Joe got his nickname from the speedy and decisive campaign he'd led on Guadalcanal, and was just the man to lead the battle for the port of Cherbourg. If he couldn't take it, nobody could.

Ike moved around the flags and pins, figuring out

the order of battle. He'd issue it to Lightning Joe as soon as he got it finished, and he'd tell him that if he didn't take Cherbourg in two weeks, he'd better start looking for another job.

FIVE

"I've got to get laid," Mahoney mumbled to himself as he lay in bed in a ward of the hospital in Southwick. He looked at his watch; it was a few minutes after midnight. He'd just returned to bed after a four-hour crap game in the latrine, and he'd won $1,800. He'd kept throwing sevens and elevens, and the dice weren't even his. Lady Luck had been sitting on his shoulder, and now the only thing to do with that kind of money was to go to the nearest whorehouse and get laid, because he knew he might be discharged from the hospital any day now, and sent directly to the front lines. If that happened, who knew when he might be able to get laid again? He might even get killed out there.

He lay silently in bed and tried to think of a plan. He was good at this type of strategic planning because he'd always obtained good results when he was a commando behind enemy lines in France. He hoped he could do half as well tonight. First of all, he needed to get a uniform from someplace, because he couldn't go to a whorehouse in the Army pajamas he was wearing. And secondly, he had to get out of the hospital although he knew that security was tighter than a drum.

Where could he get a uniform? The supply room. Everybody who checked into the hospital left his uniform down there, and although Mahoney had shown up in ragged French civilian clothes with a German uniform over it, plenty of guys checked in wearing their regular uniforms of the day.

Mahoney had figured out a way to get to the supply room. He'd merely go to the orderly's desk on the floor he was on, and steal a piece of paper of some kind. Then he'd carry the paper down to the supply room as though he was on official business. Upon reaching the supply room, he'd pick a lock or break through a door, and then find himself a uniform that fit. After putting it on, he'd bullshit or bribe his way out of the hospital. It should be a piece of cake for a guy like him who'd outsmarted the Gestapo at every turn in France for three months.

Mahoney rolled out of bed and put his big feet into the slippers they'd issued him five days ago when he'd checked in. He took the gray cotton bathrobe from the foot of the bed and put it on too. The sleeves were halfway up his forearms because they hadn't had a robe his size when he'd checked in.

His bed was in a bay area containing five other beds. Across the corridor was another identical bay containing six beds. The shades were drawn and the air smelled like alcohol and medicine. The only light came from the orderly's desk down the hall.

Mahoney shuffled down the hall to the orderly's desk, hearing guys snoring and mumbling. It was a ward where soldiers had been wounded in their arms or legs, and there were no serious casualties among them, although some would leave the hospital minus a limb, and get a one-way ticket back to the states.

Mahoney approached the orderly's desk, and sitting behind it was Corporal George Farlington of Los Angeles, California, a rotund fairy wearing a white uniform. He had a pink complexion, blond hair, and was reading a comic book. He looked up from it as Mahoney leaned his elbow on the rail in front of the desk.

"Hello there, Sergeant Mahoney," Farlington said with a big smile. "What can I do for you?"

"I can't sleep, Farlington. Give me a pill, will you?"

Farlington looked him up and down. "Why can't you sleep, Sergeant Mahoney?" he asked in his friendly girlish voice.

"How am I supposed to know?"

"Leg hurt?"

"No. It's just about all better, as a matter of fact."

"I noticed you limping still."

"It doesn't hardly hurt at all."

Farlington made his eyes sultry. "Something must be bothering you, Sergeant Mahoney."

"I guess so."

"Care to talk about it?"

"I don't have anything to talk about. I just want a pill to knock me out."

"Maybe strange thoughts are keeping you awake, Sergeant Mahoney."

"My thoughts aren't so strange," he replied.

"Well, maybe for *you* they're not strange," Farlington said with a grin, "but perhaps other people might think them strange."

"I doubt it."

Farlington looked toward a little room behind his desk. "Care to go in there and let me examine you?"

"Naw, I don't think that's necesary."

"There's no telling what's liable to turn up." Farlington winked.

"Can't I just have a pill?" Mahoney asked, reconnoitering Farlington's desk, looking at pieces of correspondence and forms, trying to figure out which would appear the most impressive.

"Sure you don't want me to examine you?"

"I'm sure."

"Nobody will know, if that's what you're worried about."

"That's not what I'm worried about."

"Oh? Then what *are* you worried about?"

"Not being able to sleep."

"If you let me examine you, I'm sure you'd be able to sleep well afterwards."

Mahoney frowned. "Corporal Farlington, will you cut the shit? Would you get me a pill please and stop trying to fuck me?"

"How crude you are, Sergeant Mahoney," Farlington said with regret and hurt in his voice.

Mahoney decided it was time to get tough. "Listen here, you little fruit. You'd better get me a couple of pills before I kick you right in the ass."

Farlington's face lit up. "Promise?"

Mahoney groaned and buried his face in his hand.

"Oh, all right," Farlington said. "If you're going to be that way, I'll get you the darned pills."

"It's about fucking time."

Farlington rose from the desk and turned around, opening the medicine cabinet behind him. Mahoney's hand swooped down on the desk and grabbed a handful of papers, dropping them into his bathrobe. Farlington shook two pills into a little paper cup, turned around, and gave them to Mahoney.

"Pleasant dreams," he said.

"Thanks."

"If you ever feel the need of a medical examination, I hope you'll know where to come." Farlington winked.

"I'll know."

"Good night, Sergeant Mahoney."

"Good night to you, Corporal Farlington."

Mahoney walked back down the hall toward his ward, then stopped and looked behind him. All he could see was the light from Farlington's area. He dropped the pills into the pocket of his robe, got down on his hands and knees, and crept silently back toward Farlington's desk, hugging the shadows, hoping no one would see him, because it would be very difficult to explain why he was crawling down the corridor in the middle of the night.

He approached Farlington's desk and paused, gathering his strength for the big push past Farlington's desk. He would have to be extremely silent, which meant he'd have to move very slowly. This meant there'd be plenty of time for someone to happen upon him. Well, the worst thing that could happen would be that they'd take away a stripe or two from him, but there were worse things, like not getting laid.

Mahoney crawled forward and now was in front of Farlington's desk. He could hear Farlington turning a page of his comic book. Continuing his surreptitious movement, Mahoney was glad he had cotton nightclothes and cotton slippers on, because they made no sound at all on the polished tile floor.

He turned left at the corner of Farlington's desk and proceeded into the next corridor, where there was a stairwell. Once he got to that stairwell he'd be loose as a goose. But first he had to pass an open gateway that led into the area where Farlington was sitting. If Farlington happened to look to the side while Mahoney was passing, he would see Mahoney, and then serious difficulties might arise. Farlington might call the MPs, or he might put Mahoney on report, or he might make him submit to an examination in the backroom for not calling the MPs or reporting him.

Life was fraught with difficulties, but Mahoney moved inexorably toward the gateway. When he reached it he peered around the corner and saw Farlington like a big fat apostrophe over his comic book, the simple queer bastard. Mahoney moved forward, silent as a snail.

Now he was directly in the gateway, in full view of Farlington if Farlington happened to look his way. Mahoney felt pinpricks of perspiration all over his body as he moved past the gateway. He was almost clear. Soon he'd be loose as a goose.

"Going somewhere, Sergeant Mahoney?" Farlington asked.

Mahoney froze and squinched his eyes shut. Oh-oh.

Farlington rose from his desk and walked to the gateway, crossing his arms and looking down at Mahoney. "What are you doing down there, Sergeant?"

"Who, me?" Mahoney asked helplessly.

"You wouldn't be going AWOL by any chance, would you, Sergeant Mahoney?"

Mahoney stood up and smiled sheepishly. "Naw."

"Then what were you doing down there, Sergeant Mahoney?"

Mahoney shifted from foot to foot and tried to think of something. "I was just trying to figure out how sharp you were, Farlington. And it turns out that you're pretty sharp. Congratulations." Mahoney held out his hand.

Farlington looked at it haughtily, his arms still crossed. "I think it's time for me to call the MPs," he said, moving toward his desk.

Mahoney grabbed him by the shoulder. "Oh, no, don't do that."

Farlington stopped and raised his eyebrows. "Why not? What have you ever done for me?"

"I'm a wounded front-line soldier," Mahoney pleaded. "Have mercy on me."

"What mercy have you ever had on me?"

"You're not a wounded front-line soldier, Farlington. Why should anybody have mercy on you?"

"I have my needs too, you know," Farlington said icily.

"Oh, I'm sure you do, Farlington. And I'm sympathetic, don't think I'm not."

"I believe you called me a little fruit a few moments ago, and threatened to kick me in the ass."

"Aw, I was only kidding," Mahoney said with a big shit-eating grin.

"Well, I'm afraid I didn't think it was very funny, so now if you'll remove your hand from my shoulder, I'd like to go to my desk and call the MPs."

Mahoney held his pudgy shoulder tightly. "You wouldn't do that to me, would you, Farlington?"

"Wouldn't I?"

"Please?"

"Take your hands off me this instant," Farlington said testily, "unless you want me to add assault to the AWOL rap you're going to get."

Mahoney held onto Farlington and tried to think of something. He decided that if he was going to get court-martialed for assault and AWOL, he might as well get court-martialed for bribery too. He had $1,800 in the pocket of his bathrobe, and money sometimes could extricate a fellow from a bad situation.

"Farlington," Mahoney said warmly, "how much would it cost to make you keep your mouth shut?"

Farlington looked down his pink nose at Mahoney. "Are you trying to bribe me, Sergeant?"

"I damn sure am," Mahoney replied with a grin.

"You don't have enough money to bribe me," Farlington said self-righteously.

"How about twenty dollars?" Mahoney asked.

"Twenty dollars is an insult to a man like me," Farlington said.

"Thirty?"

Farlington thought for a few moments. "You're getting warm."

"Thirty-five?"

"How about fifty?" Farlington asked.

"Fifty! Fifty dollars is a lot of money!"

"Not as much as you'll lose if they bust you down to Pfc and lock you in the stockade for a few months."

Mahoney grasped the logic of Farlington's argument, and reached into his pocket. "It's a deal," he said, taking out a small portion of the roll he carried there.

He counted out fifty dollars and handed it to Farlington, who counted the bills to make sure.

"It's all there?" Mahoney asked.

"Yes," Farlington replied, stuffing the bills into his pocket. "I'll just go back to my desk and continue reading, and as far as I'm concerned I haven't seen you since lights-out, Sergeant Mahoney."

"Thanks a lot, Farlington."

Farlington harumphed and returned to his desk. Mahoney turned and slinked down the corridor to the stairwell. He was pleased to have gotten out of that scrape so easily, since fifty dollars was only a small portion of the $1,800 he had in his pocket. Taking out the papers he'd lifted from Farlington's desk and neglected to mention to him, he opened the door to the stairwell and proceeded to descend it. His plan was to take the stairwell all the way down to the basement, where the supply room was. He'd worry about how to break into the supply room when he got there.

He descended the stairwell, passing the various floors of the building. He could have taken an elevator, but he might run into MPs in the elevator, or some orderly or nurse who knew him. This way was more roundabout, but there was less chance of getting caught. The main thing was not to get caught.

Finally he reached the basement. The sign on the door said OPERATING ROOMS, and he realized that he'd have to pass through that area, and maybe a few other areas that he didn't know about, before he'd reach the supply room in the other wing of the hospital.

He opened the door and a big MP was standing directly in front of him, a Colt .45 in the holster strapped to his belt.

"What do you want?" the MP asked, scowling.

Mahoney held the papers in the air. "I have to deliver these to Major Queensbury, you know where he is?"

"Never heard of him."

"He's down here someplace. I'll just have to look for him."

Mahoney walked past the MP and down the corridor, trying not to appear furtive. He passed a closed door that said OPERATING ROOM #8 and a few yards down the corridor on the other side: OPERATING ROOM #7. A door opened and a doctor in a bloody white gown came out, followed by two nurses. Mahoney envied the doctors in the hospital, because they got first crack at the nurses, some of whom were quite pretty. Unfortunately, the nurses were officers and they preferred to screw other officers, and not enlisted men like Mahoney. The few ugly pockmarked nurses who deigned to screw enlisted men were considered pathetic and declassé by their more fortunate sisters. A few days ago Mahoney had made a few lewd suggestions to a certain cute nurse, and she threatened to have him thrown in the stockade. That's when he'd decided that he'd have to find himself a nice congenial whorehouse if he wanted to get laid.

Mahoney turned a corner and bumped into another MP.

"Have you seen Major Queensbury around here?" Mahoney asked, thinking quickly.

"I think he went up to the fourth floor," the MP replied.

Mahoney did a double take, because he hadn't imagined that a real major Queensbury might exist. "I'd heard he came back here."

"Maybe he did, but I haven't seen him."

"I'll go look," Mahoney replied, turning away and walking down the corridor.

The double doors in front of him opened and some orderlies wheeled a patient through, evidently on their way to one of the operating rooms. Doctors and nurses in white uniforms followed the soldier, and Mahoney hugged the wall to let them pass, holding the papers in a conspicuous position.

He drank from a water cooler and pushed through another set of double doors. On the side of the corridor was a sign that said LATRINE; he went in and took a leak. Leaving the latrine, he hooked a left and walked down the corridor. Halfway to the next double doors he saw a door with a sign that said: DOCTORS ONLY. He looked back and forth in the corridor and didn't see anybody, so he opened the door, and his eyes bugged out when they fell on officers' uniforms on hangers in a pipe rack. No one was in the room so he dashed to the pipe rack and checked out the uniforms quickly. A couple of them looked like they might fit him so he selected the one that was largest, took the pants off the hanger, and put them on. The pants fit okay in length, but the waist was a little too big.

He put on the officer's shirt and jacket, noting that that there were captains' bars on the epaulettes. There were some brown low-quarter shoes on the floor and he put the biggest pair on, although he had no stockings. The collar of his shirt wasn't buttoned and his tie was askew, but he figured he'd better get the hell out of that room and worry about those things later. Some hats were on a rack and he selected a soft cuntcap with captains' bars on it, snatching it down and returning to the door.

He opened the door cautiously and looked into the corridor. Not a soul was there. Leaving the room, he walked down the corridor, adjusting his collar and tie. He pushed through another set of double doors, and an MP standing on the other side snapped to attention and saluted. Mahoney casually threw him a highball and walked by, thinking that was the first time in his life that he'd been saluted, and it made him feel pretty good. No wonder officers strutted around like peacocks, being saluted like that all the time.

He came to the elevators and pushed the button. A pretty young brunette nurse with green eyes and a friendly smile approached from the other end of the corridor and stopped beside the elevator.

"Good evening, doctor," she said.

"Good evening," Mahoney replied, trying to make his voice grave in the manner of doctors.

"Have a busy night?"

"Afraid so. You?"

"Uh huh."

The elevator came and they both got on. Mahoney pressed the button for the first floor, and the nurse stood in a corner of the elevator; evidently she was going to the first floor too. Mahoney thought about coming on with her because she was extremely pretty, but decided that might not be a prudent idea.

The elevator stopped on the main floor of the hospital and Mahoney stood to the side so that the nurse could get out.

"Have a nice night," he said.

"You too, doctor."

She walked down a side corridor, and he proceeded to the front door of the hospital, opening it and walking down the steps. Two more MPs saluted him, and he saluted back, feeling better as every moment passed. It was nice to be an officer. MPs salute you instead of dragging you into a doorway and asking to see your pass, and pretty nurses asked whether you had a busy night. He'd love to have a busy night with that nurse. She could sit on his face for the rest of his life, and he wouldn't mind at all.

He turned to the right and walked along casually.

A road made a big circle in front of the hospital, and halfway around the circle was a bus stop and two benches. A few officers and nurses were there already, waiting for the bus, and he decided not to sit on the benches with them because that might lead to a conversation in which they might realize that he was a fraud and an AWOL.

So he hung back a little, pacing back and forth and wishing he had a cigar. As soon as he reached London he'd buy a box of them and smoke to his heart's content. Then he'd look for a good whorehouse. He'd heard of one called Countess Lulu's off Regent Street in Soho, and intended to check it out first.

The khaki bus appeared at the bottom of the hill and climbed up slowly, making its way around the circle and stopping in front of the benches. The doctors and nurses got on, and Mahoney followed them. He wished he had stolen a visored hat because he could cover his face with it, but it was too late to worry about that mission now. He walked to the rear of the bus and sat down, far from the others who'd crowded at the front of the bus, anxious to get off fast and mess around once they hit London. He wondered if he was being conspicuous sitting back there all by himself, but nobody turned around and said anything, so he figured he was okay.

The problem was that the bus didn't leave. It just sat there with the motor running and the door opened, waiting for more passengers. Mahoney figured that it was ahead of schedule, and it was just his luck to be at the back of the bus like a sitting duck, AWOL and impersonating an officer. If they caught him it would be very serious, but they wouldn't give him the firing squad or anything like that. He'd won the DSC in North Africa and an oak leaf cluster in Italy, and the Army normally didn't shoot people like him. They just took away your stripes and sent you to the stockade for a while, or directly to the front lines. Either way, it would be worth it for a little pussy.

More doctors and nurses left the building and boarded the bus, and Mahoney looked at his watch impatiently. He hoped none of them would sit next to him because somebody might ask him a few questions and find out that he was there on a humbug.

The bus was about half full and nobody came on for a few minutes. Then he saw a figure leave the building and run down the sidewalk toward the bus. It was a nurse and she climbed onto the bus, walking toward the back. He recognized her as the one he'd seen in the elevator, and she smiled at him. He smiled back. She walked up to him.

"You saving that seat for anybody?" she asked.

"No," Mahoney replied.

"Mind if I sit down?"

"Not at all," he replied gallantly. "Would you like to sit next to the window?"

"No, that's all right," she replied, plunking herself down on the aisle seat.

Mahoney didn't know whether to feel happy about this new development or not. On one hand she was a beautiful young woman, and she certainly looked a little frisky, but on the other hand she might figure out that he was an AWOL and a lowlife, and start screaming for the MPs.

The driver closed the door and shifted into gear. The bus began moving forward. The driver steered around the circle and headed down the hill. Mahoney looked back at the hospital with most of its lights out, and hoped he'd make it back before the orderlies started their rounds in the morning.

"Why are you wearing pajamas under your uniform?" the brunette nurse asked.

"Huh?" Mahoney said, completely taken by surprise.

"I said why are you wearing pajamas under your uniform?"

Mahoney looked at her, and his teeth nearly started chattering. "What makes you think I'm wearing pajamas under my uniform?" he asked weakly.

"Because the collar of your pajamas is sticking out from underneath the collar of your shirt."

"Oh," he replied, feeling around the collar with his fingers and tucking the pajamas back in. "Well, what do you know about that?"

"I noticed it when we were in the elevator, and I said to myself: 'Shirley, I wonder why that Captain is wearing his pajamas underneath his uniform.' So I thought I'd ask you."

He looked at her, and she reminded him a little of Linda Darnell. She wore her little cap at a jaunty angle and her breasts looked pert and cute. His crotch started to get warm, but his mind was working and he thought of an alibi.

"I got an emergency call when I was home sleeping, and I got dressed without bothering to take my pajamas off," he said.

"Oh. Well, that makes sense."

"You know how it is when you get an emergency call."

She laughed sweetly. "Oh, I know all right. Once I had an emergency call and I got dressed so fast I forgot to put my underwear on."

Mahoney nearly came in his pants at the sound of that. He imagined her sitting next to him without any underwear on, and his heart started pumping furiously. "I certainly hope you're wearing underwear right now."

She fluttered her eyelashes. "Of course I am, doctor. What kind of emergency call did you get?"

"Somebody was dying."

"What of?"

"Wounds."

"What kind of wounds?"

"Stomach wounds."

"Are you a surgeon?"

"Um . . . yes."

"Where did you go to college?"

"Um . . . Fordham."

"Oh, you're from New York. I thought I detected something peculiar about your accent."

Mahoney smiled. "Well, we don't consider it so peculiar in New York. Where are you from?"

"A little town in Michigan. I'm sure you've never heard of it."

"Oh," Mahoney replied, wondering what he should say next. He looked out the window of the bus, at the streetlights and buildings they passed. "Nice night, isn't it?"

"Yes. A lovely night." Her shoulder touched his as she leaned toward the window and looked out. "I love London, don't you?"

"It's a very nice city."

"The people are wonderful, aren't they? I mean, they've been bombed so much and they're still cheerful and optimistic. They just dig themselves out and set to work rebuilding everything."

"Very nice people," Mahoney agreed.

"Do you live in the B.O.Q.?" she asked, referring to the Bachelor Officers Quarters.

"Yes, do you?"

"Uh huh, but not the same one you live in."

"Shucks," he said.

She smiled. "Do you have a wife back in the States?"

"No, do you?"

She laughed. "No, I don't have a wife back in the States."

"You know what I mean."

"I don't have a husband either."

"A boyfriend?"

She smiled poignantly. "Yes, he's in the Navy—a pilot. He's on an aircraft carrier somewhere in the Pacific Ocean. The *Gambier Bay*."

"When'd you see him last?"

"About a year and a half ago."

Little wheels began to spin in Mahoney's head. If she hadn't seen her boyfriend in a year and a half, that meant the poor little thing must be literally sex-starved. On the other hand, if she *had* been screwing other guys during that interval of time, perhaps she'd screw Master Sergeant Clarence J. Mahoney too?

"Your name is Shirley?" he asked.

"Yes, what's yours?"

"Joe," he lied.

"Joe?"

"That's right."

"What's your last name?"

"Riley," Mahoney said, thinking of his old Yorkville pal, Joe Riley.

"You're Irish?"

"As Pat Murphy's pig."

"That means you're a Catholic."

"Well, I used to be."

"I used to be an Episcopalian."

"It's hard to take that stuff seriously anymore."

She frowned. "Yes, if there was a God, I'm sure he wouldn't let things like this war happen."

"That's the way I see it."

"But of course, God didn't start the war. People did."

"That's true," Mahoney said.

"People blame God for everything that goes wrong, but when something goes right they take the credit themselves."

Mahoney raised an eyebrow. "I think you're more of an Episcopalian than you think."

She shrugged. "Maybe I am."

The bus drove into downtown London, and the streets were deserted this time of night except for an occasional group of soldiers or sailors making their way from pub to pub. Mahoney had been to London several times, and thought it a beautiful quaint old city, but he didn't know his way around very well. He had become an admirer of tall lean Englishwomen who were cold as ice until you got alone with them someplace, and kissed them on their necks a few times. Then they became hotter than the tea they served in the afternoon. He looked at the brunette sitting next to him, the shape of her crossed legs visible underneath her khaki skirt. She was giving him a hard-on, and he thought what the hell, I might as well take a shot.

"Got time to have a drink with me?" he asked, trying to sound as friendly and nonlecherous as possible.

She looked at him and thought for a few moments. "I really don't think I should."

"Why not?"

"Well, you know, I have a boyfriend, and it wouldn't be right I don't think."

"It'd just be a friendly drink."

"No, I don't think so."

"We could relax and maybe have a few laughs."

She looked at him skeptically. "That's what they all say."

He smiled. "I don't know what they all say, but when I say something you can build a house on it."

"I bet."

"It's the truth. We happen to be in London together, there happens to be a war on, and we might as well relax with each other and maybe have a few laughs, for who knows, life is short and anything could happen tomorrow."

She looked him in the eye. "Are you really a doctor?" she asked.

He was taken aback by the suddenness of her question. "What do you mean?"

"I've never met a doctor like you."

"Well, every doctor is different, I suppose."

"That's true in a way, but in another way, all doctors are alike. But you're very different."

"I am?"

"Do you know who you remind me of?"

"Who?"

"John Garfield in one of those gangster movies where he's trying to act nice to the girl."

Mahoney felt a chill in his heart. She was getting wise to him. "Nobody's ever said that to me before," he said with a false jovial note in his voice.

"What is a cardiac sphincter?"

"A what?" he asked, starting to panic.

"A cardiac sphincter."

Mahoney had no idea what that was, and knew the jig was up. He turned to her and said. "Listen, I'm not a doctor, but don't call the MPs, okay? I'm just an old dogfaced soldier and I'm going into town for a few hours to have some fun, because they're going to send me back to the front pretty soon, and you know, I might get killed out there."

She looked at him, and her eyes went soft. "I won't say anything," she said.

"Thanks a lot. I really appreciate it."

"You poor guy," she said, placing her hand on his.

Mahoney stiffened his spine. "I'm not a poor guy," he replied staunchly. "I won $1,800 tonight in a crap game in the latrine.

She burst into laughter. "You didn't!"

"Didn't I?" He reached into his pocket, took out the roll, and showed it to her. "Look."

Her eyes widened. "My goodness."

"There's nothing poor about me, lady."

"I guess not."

"Anyway, after I won it I decided to go into town and spend it, because I know they won't let me take it to the front."

"You'd probably lose it all in another crap game anyway." She touched her forefinger to his sleeve. "Where'd you get the uniform?"

He shrugged. "I stole it."

"You didn't!"

"Yes, I did."

"Where'd you steal it from?"

"I don't know, some room in the hospital."

She looked at his face more closely. "You're really something, aren't you?"

He winked. "So are you."

"Who are you really?"

"Master Sergeant Clarence J. Mahoney, Twenty-Third Rangers."

"Why were you in the hospital?"

"I got shot in the leg in France about a week ago. But I'm just about all better now."

"So fast?"

"Well, it's not a hundred percent better, but I can get around on it all right."

"Doesn't it hurt?"

"Not that much."

She shook her head slowly. "You really *are* something. Aren't you worried about getting caught?"

"What's the point of worrying about it? If they're going to get me, they're going to get me. I'll do my best to make sure they don't get me, but if they do, so what? What can they do to me? They'll bust me down again and maybe lock me up for a while. I don't care about that. You know, I'm in the kind of outfit where I really can't say for sure that I'll be alive tomorrow morning, so I figure I might as well have my fun while I can."

She thought about that, then nodded. "Yes, you have your fun, Sergeant Mahoney. Have as much fun as you can, because you deserve it I'm sure."

She placed her hand on his and squeezed it for reassurance, then returned her hands to her lap. She was so pretty and nice that Mahoney realized he was falling in love with her, but he thought that she was a nice girl and he didn't deserve her. He decided not to make any passes at her. When the bus stopped he'd just tip his hat and say good night like a gentleman. Then he'd go to Countess Lulu's in Soho and fuck his brains out.

She turned to him. "What did you do before they drafted you?"

"They didn't draft me," he replied. "I'm Regular Army."

"Oh? For how long?"

"A little over ten years."

"Why'd you join the Army ten years ago? There wasn't a war on then."

"No, but there was a Depression, and I couldn't get a job."

"Oh."

"You got a cigarette on you by any chance?" he asked.

"No, I don't smoke."

"That's good. Don't start. It's bad for you. It cuts your wind."

"Why don't you quit smoking if you believe that?"

He chuckled. "I have to face things much worse

than cigarettes, so cigarettes don't seem so bad in comparison."

"This damn war!" she said angrily, hitting her fist on her knee.

"It's a hell of a thing, isn't it?"

"It turns everybody's life upside down."

"It's best not to think too far ahead. Just take it one day at a time. That's the way I look at it."

The bus began slowing down. Mahoney looked out the window and didn't know where he was. There were tall buildings and bright lights, so he figured they were in downtown London.

"Is he gonna stop?" Mahoney asked.

"Yes," Shirley replied. "We all get out here and take other buses to our respective destinations."

"Where's here?"

"This is Shaftsbury Avenue, very close to Piccadilly Circus. You don't know London very well?"

"No."

"There are a lot of nice pubs in this area."

"Then I won't have to go far, will I?"

"You certainly won't."

The bus stopped on a street corner, and everybody in it stood up. The driver opened the door and they all filed out. Shirley left before Mahoney, putting her umbrella up against the drizzle, and he stopped onto the sidewalk, looking at a row of stores closed down for the night.

The others walked in various directions, or stood close to the building and waited for another bus. Shirley stood on the sidewalk under her umbrella, holding it high in the air so Mahoney could get under it a little. A group of British sailors passed by, drunk and rowdy.

Shirley held out her hand. "Well, good night," she said, looking into his eyes.

"He squeezed her hand gently. "Yeah, good night," he said with a smile. "Thanks for not calling the MPs."

"You're welcome. Good luck, Mahoney."

"You too, kid."

She looked down at the sidewalk and appeared uncomfortable. "It's been very nice meeting you."

"It's been nice meeting you too."

"You're a helluva guy."

"You're a helluva girl, Shirley."

She raised her face to him again, and he could see that her lips were trembling. A tear rolled down the corner of her eye, and a little cry escaped from her throat as she moved toward him. He took her in his arms, and she hugged him around the waist, her cheek coming to rest against his chest. They stood like that for a while, her umbrella dangling awkwardly behind him, and the drizzle falling on them.

Mahoney didn't know what was going on. He held her close to him and closed his eyes, feeling her young, lithe body and the tremors passing through her. Then she let him loose and pushed her dovelike hands against his chest. Her face had become blotchy and she looked disconcerted.

"Well, goodbye," she said nervously.

"Are you sure you wouldn't like to have a drink with me?" he asked, almost hoping she'd say no, so he could depart for the whorehouse immediately, and also hoping that she'd say yes, because she was sweet and good and he liked her.

"No, I don't think so," she said.

"Come on," he said, taking her arm and pulling her gently in a direction that he thought would lead to a pub.

"No . . . really . . ." she said.

"I don't think your boyfriend would mind," he lied.

"Oh, yes he would," she replied, standing under her umbrella and looking like a proper nurse again. "He's very jealous."

Mahoney looked her up and down, and grinned. "I can see why. Let's have a drink someplace, and stop worrying about your boyfriend so much. He's there and you're here. You don't have to stop living just because he's not around."

She looked up into his eyes. "I wouldn't want to get in your way, Mahoney."

"What are you talking about?"

"I know that you want to go out and have some fun, and I'm afraid I won't be very much fun for you."

"Why not?"

"You know why not."

"No, I don't. Tell me."

"Well," she said, embarrassed, "you want to find some woman to sleep with I suppose, and that's not going to be me."

He chuckled. "You're right, I'm not going to lie to you. But we've got time for a drink, what the hell."

She smiled. "No, you're just being polite." She

waved. "Go ahead and find yourself someone to sleep with. There's supposed to be a very nice cathouse on Regent Street that all the soldiers go to. It's called Countess Lulu's."

"I've heard of the place, but I'd like to have a drink with you first."

"That's not a good idea."

"Just one drink?" he asked.

"Aw Mahoney, you don't have to."

"I know I don't have to, I want to. I like you."

"I'm not going to change my mind and go to bed with you, Mahoney. I hope that's not what you're thinking."

"Of course that's not what I'm thinking."

"You sure you really want to?"

"Yes, I really want to. What do I have to do, stand on my head to prove it to you?"

"Okay, I'll have a drink with you," she said, "but if you change your mind and want to go to Countess Lulu's in a big rush, that's all right. Just tell me and I'll leave."

"Where's a nice place where I can take you?"

"The lounge of the Albemarle Hotel isn't far away. A lot of the officers go there. They've even got a little dance floor and a band."

"Sounds great. Let's go."

He took her arm and they walked over the rainy sidewalks of London. Streetlights made rippled lines on the wet pavement, and neon lights made splotches of red and green. They passed more groups of sailors and soldiers, and occasionally a serviceman walking with his arm around the shoulders of a woman. Mahoney's practiced eyes told him that most of the women were prostitutes.

"It's not much farther," Shirley said.

"I could walk with you like this forever," Mahoney replied.

She smiled. "That's an awfully sweet thing to say, Mahoney."

"It's the truth."

"It is not the truth. You can't wait to get to Countess Lulu's."

"Sure I can."

"You know, you've really turned out to be a big surprise, Mahoney. you appear to be a big tough guy, but you're really very gentle and soft."

"I am not soft!" Mahoney said vehemently.

She squeezed his arm. "I didn't mean it in the sense that I thought you were weak. I just mean that you're really a gentleman, although you don't look like one."

"I don't look like a gentleman?"

"No."

"Then what do I look like?"

She laughed. "Mahoney, when I saw you in that elevator I thought you were a gangster who somehow became a doctor and wound up in the army. Then when I saw your pajamas sticking out, you really provoked my curiosity. That's why I sat beside you on the bus."

"You didn't think I was good-looking?" Mahoney asked, his vanity getting the better of him.

"You're a very attractive man in a way. I'll bet you have a lot of girlfriends."

"I'm in the Army, Shirley. I live with a bunch of guys. There ain't any women around."

"Yes, but whenever you get into a town I'm sure you do all right."

"Depends on how much money I have."

"You're awful," she said.

"Why am I awful?"

"I don't know. Maybe it's me. Maybe there's something about you that makes me want to be awful."

Mahoney's head lit up like a hundred watt bulb. "There is?"

"Don't let your imagination run away with you, Mahoney."

"Oh no, no. Of course not."

"I'm just speaking abstractly."

"Oh, sure."

"There *is* something very attractive about you."

Mahoney snorted. "What? The fact that I look like a gangster?"

"A lot of women are attracted to men who are big and tough like you, especially when they realize that you're decent guys."

"I'll tell you something, Shirley, I'm not such a decent guy."

"Sure you are."

"I'm really not."

"Well you'd better be as long as you're with me."

"You—you're practically a nun. Who could be anything else but a decent guy with you?"

"You mean I'm like the girl next door?"

"That's right."

She snatched her arm away. "I don't want to be the girl next door."

"Well, that's what you are. You might as well get

used to it."

"That's not what I am," she said angrily. "I'm a woman."

"Then you're the woman next door. The one who's in love with the Navy pilot."

"That's a little better," she said, letting him take her arm again.

They turned the corner and saw the sign of the Albemarle Hotel. Army and Navy officers were gathered in front with nurses and civilian women, and some entered and left the front door of the hotel. A cab pulled up to the hotel and discharged an Air Corps pilot and a pretty blonde. Two drunken Army officers took their places in the cab, which then drove away.

Mahoney and Shirley entered the lobby of the hotel, crowded with officers and ladies, and Mahoney drank in everything with his eyes, for he was curious about how the other military half lived, and it appeared to be living pretty good. He held Shirley's arm and they entered the lounge, which had a semicircular bar against one wall, a small dance floor in back, and tables in front. Brightly colored balloons clung to the ceiling, and the walls were wood-paneled. The lights were low and the headwaiter walked toward them, twiddling his mustache.

"A table for two," Mahoney said, reaching into his pocket.

"I'm sorry, sir, but the tables are all taken. I'm afraid you'll have to stand at the bar."

Mahoney looked at the bar and it was like Grand Central Station at five o'clock. He handed the headwaiter a twenty dollar bill. "A table for two."

"I told you sir that . . ."

Mahoney passed him another twenty. "A table for two."

"I'll see what I can do, sir."

The headwaiter walked off into the crowd, and Mahoney looked at the drunken officers and their women attempting to dance on the floor in front of the five-piece orchestra and female vocalist who was warbling:

There'll be bluebirds over
the white cliffs of Dover
tomorrow, just you wait and see . . .

Mahoney thought that Messerschmitt 109s would appear over the white cliffs of Dover before bluebirds showed up, but there was no harm in hoping.

"Penny for your thoughts," she said.

"Oh, nothing."

"You look so serious all of a sudden."

"Don't worry about it."

The headwaiter returned. "I've found a little table for the both of you," he said.

"I kind of thought you would," Mahoney replied.

The headwaiter led them into the lounge, and Mahoney glanced at his watch. It was almost two o'clock in the morning, and he had to be back to the hospital before roll call at seven. He was certain that he could get back in time and still do all that he wanted to do at Countess Lulu's.

The table was against the left wall, and it was a tiny little thing with a candle in a red glass holder and an ashtray sitting in the middle. Mahoney and

Shirley sat down, and a waitress showed up, dropping little doilies in front of each of them.

"What'll you have?" she asked, fidgeting nervously.

Mahoney looked at Shirley. "Care for some champagne?"

"That's much too expensive," she replied, her midwestern sense of frugality coming to the fore. "I'll just have a whisky and soda."

"Don't you like champagne?"

"Of course I like champagne."

Mahoney turned to the waitress. "A bottle of your best champagne, and two packages of Lucky Strikes if you've got them, and if you don't have them, two packages of whatever cigarettes you have."

The waitress disappeared into the clouds and smoke, and Mahoney looked around. "This is a real nice joint," he said.

"I think it's an abomination," she replied. "It's much too crowded and much too expensive, but there aren't many places to go."

"You should see where the enlisted men go. Those places make this one look like Sunday school."

"Really?" she asked, perking up. "What happens?"

"Fights."

"What else?"

"Basically just fights."

"Have you ever been in a fight?"

"Are you kidding?" He touched his nose. "My nose is broken right here from a fight."

"I thought it was a little crooked."

The waitress returned with a bottle of champagne

and two glasses, plus two packages of English cigarettes. She had no champagne bucket, uncorking the bottle and placing it on the table.

"Seven pounds, two shillings," the waitress said in a cockney accent.

"Mahoney looked at Shirley. "How much is that in American money?"

Shirley brought her eyes to half mast and did some computations in her mind. "Give her twenty-five dollars and tell her to keep the change."

Mahoney did so and the waitress appeared quite pleased as she walked away. He poured champagne into the two glasses and held his up in the air.

"To Countess Lulu," he said.

"I'm not drinking to Countess Lulu," Shirley snapped back.

"To Ike?"

"Okay."

They clicked glasses and sipped champagne. He gazed at her over the top of his glass, admiring the gentle curve of her nose and her nice kissable lips. Her bosom swelled nicely and he'd caught a glimpse of her cute fanny while they were crossing the lobby. She'd told him she liked him, so there was the possibility that he could seduce her. It was a long shot but worth a try, because she probably was prettier than the sleazy whores he'd find at Countess Lulu's, and he was crazy about her anyway. He looked at his watch and told himself that if he didn't get into her pants by four o'clock in the morning, he'd leave her and hotfoot it over to Countess Lulu's.

"Late for an appointment?" she asked, noticing

him looking at his watch.

"No, just checking out the time."

"Countess Lulu's is open all night, so you don't have to worry about getting there before closing time."

He opened a package of cigarettes, took one out, and lit it up. "I'm not worried about going to Countess Lulu's."

"You shouldn't have ordered a full bottle of champagne. I told you I would be happy with a plain whisky and soda. I'd finish it in fifteen minutes and then you could put me in a cab. You'd be at Countess Lulu's in under forty-five minutes."

"I'm not interested in being at Countess Lulu's in forty-five minutes." He stood and grabbed her hand. "Let's dance."

"Hey!" she said, remaining glued to her chair.

"Come on."

He pulled her to her feet and dragged her to the dance floor, noticing she wasn't resisting that much. She liked him, there was no question about that. The big question was whether she'd let him into her pants.

The dance floor was crowded and the band was playing "Don't Sit Under the Apple Tree With Anybody Else But Me." Mahoney took Shirley by the waist and hand and glided her through the other couples, but she kept her distance and their bodies weren't touching.

"I haven't danced for so long," she said nostalgically. "You dance very well for a man your size, by the way."

"Thanks."

The beat was fast and everybody was bouncing around. Other couples brushed up against them or bumped into them, and there was something frantic about it all, but Mahoney knew it was only the war, with everybody trying to squeeze each last drop of pleasure out of life, because life was so short, and anything could happen tomorrow.

The music slowed to "Stardust," and Shirley moved closer, the tips of her boobs touching his jacket when he executed certain sneaky moves. He wanted to crush her against him and fasten his mouth on hers, sucking out her beauty and sweetness, and then tear off her clothes and ravish her.

"I feel so secure with you," she said, moving closer.

"I feel very nice with you, too, Shirley."

She rested her cheek against his chest. "The war has made such a mess out of so many lives."

"That's the way it goes," Mahoney said philosophically.

"People do things that they otherwise would never do," she continued. "For instance, if it weren't for the war, I'd be married to Bob and would never be dancing with you like this, in this dark old place, with all these drunks around us."

"I guess the war has brought people closer in certain ways," he said.

"Yes, but it makes so many problems, because you know, Mahoney, I like you very much."

She brought her body to rest against his, and they danced across the stardust. He was becoming dizzy with love and lust, for he hadn't touched a woman for a while, and this Shirley was lovely and lithe, and there was a purity about her that he found enchanting.

The band broke into a languid version of "Sunrise Serenade," and Mahoney held her tightly, thinking of all the women he'd danced with in his life and all the crazy things he'd done with them afterwards, and wondered if he wasn't in his hospital bed dreaming all this, because it was preposterous really, him in a captain's uniform dancing with a lieutenant in a London hotel lounge.

She cuddled closer to him, as they swayed and turned. "I knew I shouldn't have come here with you," she said.

"I thought you just said you felt secure with me."

"I feel secure about you but I don't feel secure about me."

He thought about that for a few moments, and it only could mean one thing. The time had come for strategic maneuvers. He kissed her ear, and she shivered.

"Don't do that," she whispered.

"I'm crazy about you, Shirley."

"I'll bet you say that to all the girls."

"Only the ones I'm crazy about."

"You're probably crazy about all of them."

"No, not all of them."

She rested her cheek against his chest. "Oh, Mahoney, this war is so crazy."

"It's the craziest thing that ever happened."

"I should be married to Bob right now," she said, "and be living in Lansing, Michigan. I'd be a nurse at a hospital and he'd probably be an executive at the Oldsmobile plant. Where would you be?"

"Probably in some stockade someplace."
"You've been in the stockade before?"
"Twice."
"What for?"
"Insubordination the first time, and a fight in the mess hall the second time. Nothing too serious."
She looked up at him and said sadly. "Oh, Mahoney, what are we doing here together?"
"I don't know," he replied, kissing her cheek.
She looked frightened and she turned her lips to him, and he kissed those red berries delicately, because he didn't want to unravel his tongue down her throat and scare her away.
She pulled away from him. "I think we'd better sit down."
"Let's get a room someplace."
Her eyes widened. "Are you crazy!"
"I'm crazy about you."
"I'm engaged, Mahoney."
"There's a war on, Shirley. We have to make the best of things."
"Oh, no we don't."
They continued dancing, and she leaned her full weight against him, letting him move her around the floor. The band was playing "I'm In The Mood For Love."
"Why can't we get a room together, Shirley?"
"You know very well why."
"Tell me."
"Because I'm engaged, and because I don't want to have a cheap squalid little one-night affair with somebody I don't even know."
"Please," he said, holding her tighter.

"Don't do this to me, Mahoney," she pleaded. "I can't stand it."

"Please," he repeated.

"No."

"Tomorrow morning you can go back to being engaged, and I'll probably go back to the front, but at least tonight we can . . . you know."

"I don't want to know."

"You know you like me, Shirley."

She nodded, her cheek against his chest. "I know."

"Then why shouldn't we?"

"Because I don't want to be like all the others here, jumping into bed all the time with whoever happens to be convenient."

"Look at me, Shirley," he said.

"I don't want to look at you."

"C'mon, look at me."

He put his finger under her chin and raised her face. Their eyes met as they danced among the crowd on the floor.

"The whole world is turned upside down," he said, "and a person's life isn't worth a dime. There's no guarantee that our side will even win the war. So we might as well take whatever happiness we can find and be glad that we got it, because there's so much misery and confusion around."

"I know you're right," she replied, "but I just can't do it. I'm not that kind of a person."

He shrugged. "I'm not going to try and talk you into it. If you don't want to, you don't want to."

"It's not that I don't want to," she said, placing her cheek against his chest again. "It's that I can't . . . because of Bob. I'd never be able to look him in the eye again."

"How do you know what he's doing right now?"

"Don't say that, Mahoney."

"His aircraft carrier might be in port right now, and he might be lonely. Would you get mad if he found a girl to keep him company for a few hours?"

"Of course not."

"Do you think he'd feel any different if you did something like that?"

She looked at him again. "Mahoney, I think it's time you went to Countess Lulu's."

"Is that what you really think?"

"I'm afraid so."

"Okay."

They separated and walked off the dance floor, returning to their table. Mahoney put his two packs of cigarettes into his jacket pocket and picked up his hat.

"Aren't you going to finish your champagne?" she asked.

"To hell with the champagne. Let's go."

They made their way through the sea of tables and revelers to the door of the lounge.

"Are you mad at me?" she asked.

"Of course not."

"You sure?"

"Completely sure."

"I don't want you to be mad because you know that I really do like you."

"I know."

"If it weren't for Bob and my moral upbringing, I'd probably do whatever you wanted me to do."

Mahoney nodded. They left the lounge and crossed the lobby of the hotel, passing through the open door and descending the steps in front to the sidewalk. It was still drizzling, and there were fewer people hanging around in front.

"I'll get you a cab," Mahoney said, looking both ways into the street.

"I'll probably get home faster if I catch the bus. Why don't you walk me to the bus stop—it's on the way to Countess Lulu's."

"Okay."

He lit a cigarette, the glow of the match illuminating his rugged features, and walked beside her toward the bus stop. A solitary occupied cab drove down the street, and a GI was passed out in the doorway of a tailor shop.

"Are you mad at me?" she asked.

"No, I'm not mad at you."

"I think you are."

"I'm really not."

"Well, you've certainly become cool."

He looked at her and puffed his cigarette. "Well, there's no point in staying hot, is there?"

"No."

"All right, then."

They continued down the street and turned left at the corner. He felt tired and a little disappointed, but he'd done his best and couldn't reproach himself for anything. If she wanted to remain true to her boyfriend in the South Pacific who probably was screwing some Filipino broad right now, it was all right with him. He'd just go to Countess Lulu's and get his rocks off that way. But he'd sure like to crawl into a bed someplace with Shirley.

She took his arm. "Do you know when they're going to discharge you from the hospital?"

"In another day or two, I guess."

"What then?"

"My outfit is fighting in France. I guess I'll rejoin them."

"You must be a little afraid of all that."

"A little, but General Patton spoke to us once and he said the best way to deal with fear is to concentrate on following orders and trying to do your duty, and that's the way I handle it, I guess. When they say charge I charge, and when they say dig in I dig in. If they tell me to take a particular objective I try to take it. That's about it."

"I've noticed you limping a little. Is your leg all right?"

"Just about. It wasn't a bad wound. I got a bad one in Italy, though. A stomach wound. But they got all the shrapnel out and I didn't lose too much of my guts."

"I hope you'll be all right, Mahoney."

"It don't matter to me either way," he replied, puffing his cigarette. "If a bullet comes with your name on it, there's nothing you can do except go down like a soldier."

She looked at him. "I'll bet you're a good soldier."

"As a matter of fact, I am a pretty good soldier. That's because I really don't give a shit, you know what I mean?"

"Don't you want to live? Don't you like life?"

"Yeah, I like life I guess. But I'm not crazy about

it. I mean, what is it? A struggle to survive, that's all. Whether you're in the Army or back in New York, it's just a struggle to survive."

She shrugged. "I've never seen life as a struggle like that."

"Maybe that's because you never had to struggle very much."

"As a matter of fact I never have."

"Thank your lucky stars that you haven't," he said, "and pray that you never have to."

They approached the bus stop, and a few male and female officers were there. Mahoney looked at his watch; it was two-thirty in the morning. He'd have plenty of time for an orgy at Countess Lulu's.

"Well, here we are," Shirley said.

Mahoney nodded. "Yup." He held out his hand. "Well, good night."

"Aren't you going to kiss me good night?"

"If you want me to."

She reached for him. "You know I want you to."

They were standing close to a red brick building, and he took her in his arms. Her face was upturned and her eyes a little frightened as he closed the distance and kissed her lips. They were soft and small, and she whimpered as she opened them to admit his hungry tongue. He lowered his hands to her fanny and pulled her tight against his erection; she didn't try to get away from it. He felt her fingernails in his shoulders as her body strained against him. I think I've got her now, Mahoney's reeling mind told him.

She had been on her tiptoes, and now dropped down again, looking at his face. Her eyes were wide and wild.

"What do I see in you?" she asked.

"Let's get a room someplace," he replied.

She closed her eyes and sighed. "I don't know about anything anymore."

"Stop thinking, let me think for both of us," he said. "Take my hand and let's go."

He took her little hand in his and started walking. She walked beside him as though in a daze.

"I think I'm losing my mind," she said. "Where are we going?"

"To the first decent hotel we can find."

"I know where there's one."

"You mean the Albemarle?"

"No, another one. It's just a few blocks from here. I've been there before. Don't ask me who I was there with, but I've been there before."

His head jerked in surprise. "You've been there before with someone else?"

"Isn't that what I just said?"

"But . . . what about Bob?"

She stopped and looked up at him. She was so pretty and so utterly vulnerable that he wanted to pick her up and cuddle her like a baby.

"I try to be a good person," she said softly, "but I get lonely and crazy sometimes, and then I meet one of you big beautiful doomed bastards, and I just fall in love with you. Oh, I don't know if it's real love or not, or if it's pity or just plain old lust, and I don't want it to happen, but finally I give in. I'm weak I guess."

"Which way's that hotel?" Mahoney asked.

"Is that all you can say?"

"I think its location has become sort of important."

"Kiss me first."

They hugged and kissed as the rain fell lightly upon them. Mahoney was delirious with joy and passion as he felt the ribs of her back, and tasted her sweet mouth. She nibbled his tongue and pressed her body against him, holding nothing back.

She sighed and pressed her face against his chest. "When I saw you on the bus, I knew I was lost," she said. "I've always been attracted to John Garfield types. So I sat down beside you like a little slut. You must have thought I was awful."

"I thought you were terrific, as a matter of fact."

"Did you think I'd be an easy lay?"

"No, I thought you'd be impossible."

"Impossible?" She laughed sardonically. "No, I'm not impossible. I'm just another Army nurse who's being unfaithful to her boyfriend."

He placed his forefinger on her nose. "Stop that."

"It's the truth."

"It's not the truth. The truth is that the war is driving everybody nuts. It's even driving me nuts, and I was nuts long before I ever joined the Army."

"You're not even an officer."

"I'm a master sergeant, and that's better than an officer."

She laughed again, more happily this time. "I think you're marvelous, Mahoney."

"Where's that hotel?"

She took his hand and they walked through the deserted rainy streets. Mahoney thought of how nice it would be if he could live with Shirley, and maybe be married to her. It would be wonderful to come home to someone like her every night, but instead they'd just have a few hours in a hotel room, and a week from now Germans would be shooting at him, and she might be heading for this hotel with another lonely GI.

The hotel was on a side street and was called the Selridge. It looked genteel and illicit at the same time. They climbed the steps and entered the small lobby that had a worn carpet on the floor and worn old furniture positioned upon it. The lobby smelled like an attic that no one had cleaned for years.

The clerk was an elderly man wearing pince-nez glasses, and he behaved in a friendly manner as he went through the formalities of the check-in. Mahoney thought the old guy might have been a soldier once himself, and signed a fictitious name on the register. He accepted the keys to the room and followed Shirley up the stairs, looking at her long, slim legs, wanting to stop and kiss them.

The room was on the fourth floor, and he unlocked the door, walking toward the bed and turning on the lamp on the night table. The room was run-down, but warm and cozy. He returned to the door, closed and latched it.

"Well, here we are," he said dropping the keys onto a sagging dresser.

She wrinkled her nose. "What a dump."

Mahoney was taking off his jacket. "It looks fine to me."

She removed her hat. "It's so squalid."

"I don't think so."

"What would you know? You were on your way to Countess Lulu's."

"Countess Lulu's is supposed to be a first-class joint."

“I wouldn’t know, I’ve never been there.”

“I should hope not.” Unknotting his tie, he walked to the window and pulled the shade. “That’s better.”

She unbuttoned her jacket. “Well, at least it’s a cheaper deal for you here.”

Frowning, he moved toward her and held her shoulders. “I realize this isn’t much, Shirley, but let’s make the most of it.”

She looked into his eyes. “But it’s all so . . . so sordid in a way, do you know what I mean?”

“I know it’s not the bridal suite at the Waldorf-Astoria, but the bridal suite at the Waldorf-Astoria never had a bride more beautiful than you.”

She closed her eyes and kissed his throat. “That was so nice, Mahoney.”

“It’s the truth.”

“I’m sure the bridal suite at the Waldorf-Astoria never had a groom more gallant than you.”

“I don’t know about that,” he said, kissing her forehead.

“I’m absolutely convinced of it. In fact I’m very happy to be here with you, and I mean it.”

“I’m glad, because I’ve been through a lot of ups and downs with you during the past few hours.”

“I’m sorry. Sometimes I get confused.”

“It’s all right.”

“Put out the light, will you, Mahoney?”

“Sure.”

He walked in long strides to the lamp and clicked it off, plunging the room into darkness. His eyes adjusted as he peeled off his shirt, and in the light of the streetlamp he could see Shirley folding her service blouse over a chair. Her skin was white and ghostly, and her face like a marble statue. She stepped out of her skirt and she had a lovely figure in her bra and underpants, with larger breasts than he'd thought. With trembling hands he tore off the clothes he'd stolen, and then his pajamas. She was unhooking her brassiere when he moved to her, touching her shoulders with his hands, and kissing her forehead. She removed the brassiere and pressed against him, and he thrilled at the touch of her nipples against his chest.

She was soft and warm, yet firm and strong. They found each other's lips and feasted hungrily. He ran the palms of his hands down her body and gripped the round cheeks of her rump, and she pressed her belly against his big throbbing erection.

"You're such a big man," she whispered into his ear.

"Let's go to bed."

Awkward and a little embarrassed, she took the few steps across the floor to the bed, got into it, and lay on her back. Naked, he lay on top of her, an artery in his neck throbbing, his heart beating like a tom-tom. He wrapped his arms around her, and she seemed so frail underneath him. He kissed her hairline, her cheek, and her lips. His head was spinning and he wished he had more lips and more hands, because he wanted to do everything, and all at once. He licked her tongue, then kissed her neck and soft white throat. Moving lower, he kissed the warm place between her breasts, and then moved to her nipple, taking it into his mouth and sucking it as she sighed and moved her head from side to side on the pillow. He sucked her other breast, then put both nipples into his mouth and slavered them with his tongue. Her chest heaved and her stomach quivered. He rolled off her and pulled down her underpants; she raised her legs to help him get them off.

Now she was naked, and so was he. He kissed her again and extended his tongue into her mouth, slurping her up, while burrowing his fingers into the slippery place between her legs. She undulated like the waves of an ocean and he inserted his finger inside, feeling the little fleshy pebbles in her most hidden place. She bit his cheek and then his ear. Her fingernails dug into his shoulder, and she murmured "oh my God I can't believe it."

He rolled on top of her and she spread her legs. He took his dick in hand and moved it toward her valley of dreams, but she whispered wait a minute, and touched it with her hand, running her fingers over its tender head, and he thought he'd faint from the gloriousness of it all. Then she took her hand away and he sank it in slowly, savoring every inch of penetration, and whispering into her ear that he loved her.

She wrapped her long legs around his hips, and he started to work her slowly, because he wanted it to last. She bit his chin gently and made growling feminine sounds in her throat, and he held her cute ass, pushing in and pulling out of her juicy goodness. She scratched her fingernails across his back, but he didn't mind. He wouldn't care if she ripped him apart, as long as she let him continue to do what he was doing.

He moved up her body so the top of his dick ran

across her little jellybean whenever he moved in or out. Her eyes rolled into her head when he made contact and she said, "you're going to kill me." He replied that he had no such intention.

They held each other tightly and humped like wild animals. Their gasps and moans echoed around the little room, merging with the sound of an occasional vehicle outside, and a drunken GI strolled past singing:

Would you like to swing on a star
Carry moonbeams home in a jar?

Mahoney felt himself coming. He wanted to hold it off for a while longer, but he was on fire and far beyond any hope of self-control. It began as a tickle somewhere down in his soul and the movement of his hips became erratic as he raised his face from her neck.

"Don't come inside me!" she whispered frantically.

He yanked it out and she seemed to deflate like a balloon that had been punctured. Dropping onto her, he laid it on her stomach and exploded hot cream all over her. She hugged him tightly against her and they screwed that way as his dam burst again and again, and he wished he'd worn a rubber so he could have come inside her, but no, doing it with a rubber was like washing your feet with your socks on, and he'd wanted to feel her, know her, and love her without anything between them.

"I think I'm going to drown," she said, breathing heavily. "My period will be here in just a few days. I probably can't get pregnant now anyway."

"This is a helluva time to tell me that."

"I just thought of it." She pinched his ass. "I wasn't thinking too clearly a few moments ago."

He rolled onto his side, and she touched his dick. It still was hard as a rock.

"Gee," she said, "most men get soft after they have an orgasm, but you don't. You're really special, Mahoney, you know that?"

"I'm just an ordinary dogface, baby."

"No, you're not. You're really not." She sucked in air through her clenched teeth as she caressed his dick and jerked him off a little. "It feels so good. Let's do it some more."

"Take your hand away."

"I can't."

"We can't do it anymore if you don't take your hand away."

"Oh, all right."

She took her hand away and he crawled on top of her, jabbing his dick in again. Sighing, her eyes rolling back into her head, she spread her legs wantonly and worked her hips, while he pumped her and thought of how demure she'd been when they were riding in the bus, and what a passionate little devil she was now. He'd never have guessed it, and he imagined it was that way with most women: they were quite ordinary when you saw them on the street, and you'd never dream that when they were in bed they fucked like wildcats.

He positioned himself again so that his dick rubbed her jellybean, because he knew that's the way women liked it best.

"Oh," she said, nibbling his lips.

He moved faster and held her ass for leverage. Her

head fell back and she looked up at him, her face contorted in the light of the streetlamp.

"OH!" she said again.

He knew he had her coming now, and he loved to make women come. They went out of their minds and lost control of themselves completely, scratching and biting, with all their fancy hoity-toity manners on the floor with their clothes.

"OH!"

She kicked her legs in the air and bucked like a bronco. Mahoney wrapped one arm around her shoulders, cradled her fanny with his other arm, and fucked her with a vengeance.

"OH-OH-OH-OH . . . "

She dug her fingernails into his back and he almost cried out in pain as he kept working her. She pinched her lips together and tried to stop from screaming, but sound erupted anyway as the big electrical current was switched on inside her. She went into sexual convulsions, gasping for air and shaking her ass, and it was so wild that Mahoney felt himself coming again. His dick blasted loose inside her and she writhed and moaned like a forest beast as she reached around and grabbed his hairy ass, sinking her fingernails into it, the bed bouncing up and down so furiously Mahoney thought it might collapse.

He squirted into her again and again, and she clutched his ass as though she wanted to stuff his entire body into the slit between her legs. He kept humping her until he became dry, but still he kept going. Their movements slowed down and their chests heaved. Finally they lay motionless, he still inside her.

"How do you feel?" he asked, looking down at her shadowy face.

"I should feel awful, but I don't," she said. "I must be getting jaded."

"I don't know that much about your love life, dearie, so I couldn't say."

She shook her head. "No, I don't think I'm getting jaded. I really don't do it *that* much."

"How often do you do it?"

"I don't know. Maybe one night like this every two or three months."

"That's not much."

She dug her knuckles into his ribs. "Maybe it's not much to you, Mahoney, but it's a lot to me."

"I'm going to get a cigarette," he said.

He crossed the room and picked up his jacket. Taking out a package of cigarettes and a book of matches, he returned to the bed and lit one up, dropping the match into the ashtray beside him. He lay on his back with his head on the pillow and she snuggled against him kissing his shoulder.

"What's this?" she asked, touching a scar.

"There's where a bullet went in."

"You poor bastard, Mahoney."

"Nobody who's ever been to bed with you can be called a poor bastard."

She kissed the scar. "You always say the right thing."

He puffed the cigarette and looked at the ceiling. It was hard for him to believe there was a war going on out there.

SIX

A German platoon advanced cautiously up the street of a small coastal village several miles to the northwest of St. Mère Eglise. They were part of an engineer battalion attacking the village and making good progress against a numerically inferior and exhausted American force.

The platoon leader was Lieutenant Rudolf Schmidt, a stocky black-haired officer who held an engineering degree from the University of Breslau. He excelled at leading troops in demolitions, building bridges, and laying mine fields, and was a good engineering officer, but actual combat was not his forte, and he proceeded with his platoon down the street cautiously, perhaps too cautiously, because troops moving slowly make good targets.

His platoon turned a corner, looking into the windows of houses for any movement that would indicate the presence of the enemy. Lieutenant Schmidt motioned with his arms for his platoon to spread out, so that one hand grenade or mortar shell wouldn't kill them all at once. Hunched over, his rifle in his hands and his brown eyes scrutinizing everything, he led his platoon into the new street, poised to move for cover at the first sign of danger.

He heard the report of a rifle, and a bullet whistled past his ear, striking a soldier behind him.

"Take cover!" Lieutenant Schmidt screamed.

His soldiers dashed into doorways and behind trees as a barrage of rifle fire erupted in their midst. Schmidt dropped to his belly behind a lamp post and looked around it to see where the fire was coming from. He saw puffs of smoke erupting from a house down the street, and he'd received enough infantry training to realize that the only thing to do was attack.

He shouted to his squad sergeants and told them what to do. One would take his squad around and attack the house from the rear. Another would attack the house from the right flank. He would lead the remaining two squads on a frontal rush. They'd stay in touch through their field radios, and the two sergeants would notify Schmidt when they were in position.

Schmidt and his two squads poured fire into the house as the other two squads moved out. He saw one American soldier try to fire back, and the American's face was ripped apart by bullets as he fell back out of sight. Schmidt saw his two enveloping squads jumping fences and running into alleys and they moved to their positions. In the middle of the street he saw the soldier who'd been hit by the first shot; he was moaning softly but not moving a muscle.

The calls from the two sergeants came in over the field radio, and Schmidt's runner reported that they were in position. There was nothing further to wait for, so Schmidt told his runner to order them to attack. Then he raised his rifle in the air and told the two squads with him to charge the house. He scrambled to his feet and led the charge, firing as he went, because junior officers in the German Army were trained to take the initiative and get in front of an attack where their troops could see them.

Unfortunately, that made him a prime target for the Americans, so his mouth was dry and his teeth chewed the flesh inside his mouth. He ran down the street toward the house. He heard fire coming from the rear and right flank of the house, and American heads appeared in two of the windows but promptly were shot by Schmidt's advancing squads. Sergeant Hettel darted forward on the right side of the skirmish line and hurled a hand grenade through one of the house's windows. It exploded and Schmidt lobbed a grenade at the front door, falling to the pavement as it blew apart.

"CHARGE!" Schmidt yelled.

He ran through the door and was the first one in the house. An American soldier was huddled behind a table and fired his Colt .45, but the bullet went wide of Schmidt, who fired his rifle from the hip, shooting away the soldier's jaw. Sergeant Hettel shot down another American soldier by the fireplace, and someone else shot an American behind a wooden chair that really furnished no protection at all.

Schmidt heard his other squads enter the house from their various angles, and could hear shots and explosions. His men poured into the rooms and corridors adjacent to the room he was in, and he walked cautiously, his rifle at the ready, toward the

American he'd shot behind the table, because he thought he'd seen the insignia of an officer on his collar.

Schmidt moved behind the table and saw the American soldier lying on his side. Sure enough, there was a silver bar of a first lieutenant on his shoulder, and his blond hair was stained by the widening pool of blood that he was lying in. Schmidt stepped closer and saw that the first lieutenant was about his age and looked more like an Aryan German than he himself.

Then he noticed the leather briefcase lying beside the first lieutenant. Bending to pick it up, he opened the flap and saw a sheaf of papers inside. Taking them out of the briefcase, he noticed that the front page had a military insignia on top and the words:

HEADQUARTERS
U.S. SEVENTH CORPS

Schmidt couldn't read English, but he thought the papers might be important. The first lieutenant might have been a staff courier of some kind who'd happened to be in the village when the surprise attack from Schmidt's engineer battalion had taken place. Yet on the other hand, maybe the papers weren't important at all, because surely the first lieutenant would have tried to destroy them. But maybe he hadn't had time. Maybe he'd thought he could get away.

The squad sergeant reported to Schmidt, smiling because they'd taken the house with no casualties except for the soldier who'd been wounded in the street. Schmidt told one of the sergeants to have the man evacuated to a field hospital, and the sergeant issued the appropriate orders to two of his privates.

Schmidt told the senior sergeant to take command of the platoon. "I have to take this to battalion headquarters," he explained, holding the briefcase in the air.

SEVEN

"Mein Fuehrer!" said Field Marshal Wilhelm Keitel as he entered Adolf Hitler's office at Berchtesgaden, "I have good news!"

Hitler's heavy-lidded eyes looked at his top military commander. Could it be that through some miracle the allied armies suddenly had been thrown into the sea? "What is it!"

Keitel was a tall, elegant man with a gray mustache. He advanced to Hitler's desk and took a handful of papers out of his briefcase. "This!"

Hitler furrowed his brow as he looked at the papers. "What are they?"

"The battle order for the American Seventh Corps!" Keitel said triumphantly.

Hitler arose unsteadily and looked at the papers. He had a stomachache, a headache, and an hour ago had received an injection of drugs and vitamins from his quack doctor, Theodor Morell. "Let me see them," he said, holding out his blue-veined hand.

Keitel handed the papers over and leaned toward Hitler, resting his fists on Hitler's desk. "There's very important information in here, mein Fuehrer," he said.

Hitler put on his wire-rimmed glasses and leafed through the papers. "Such as?"

"The American Seventh Corps will make an all-out attack on Cherbourg on the 15th of June, which is tomorrow!"

Hitler banged his fist on his desk. "I knew it!"

"You knew it?"

"Of course I knew it, you fool!" He pointed behind him to the huge map of Europe on the wall. "They need the port of Cherbourg to unload reinforcements, supplies, and oil."

"Well," Keitel said respectfully, "they seem to be doing rather well with the port facilities they've improvised. Are you sure they need Cherbourg that badly, mein Fuehrer?"

Hitler plopped back into his chair and narrowed his eyes at Keitel. "Keitel, you're a fool," he said.

"I am?" Keitel asked, blushing.

"You must be a fool if you don't appreciate the strategic importance of Cherbourg to Eisenhower," Hitler said. "If he wants to mount a vigorous offensive against us, he'll need more men and equipment, don't you understand?"

"My intelligence reports indicate they have plenty of men and equipment as it is," Keitel said emphatically.

"Plenty for what?" asked Hitler. "For fighting a static little beachhead war? Yes, they have plenty for that, but they want to break out of that beachhead and slash their way into the heartland of Germany! For that they will require an overwhelming superiority in men and equipment, can't you see that?"

"Yes, mein Fuehrer," Keitel said automatically,

although he still wasn't sure that Hitler was right.

"I am surrounded by fools," Hitler mumbled.

"What was that, mein Fuehrer?"

"Never mind. Who is in command of the fortress at Cherbourg right now?"

"Lieutenant-General Carl Wilhelm von Schlieben, mein Fuehrer."

"What kind of a man is this von Schlieben?" Hitler asked.

Keitel scratched his cheek. He sat in one of the chairs facing Hitler's desk and crossed his legs. He appeared to be deep in thought.

"Well?" Hitler asked impatiently.

Keitel cleared his throat. "I've always considered him to be an utter fool."

"What!" Hitler screamed.

"I'm sorry, mein Fuehrer, but I've never thought very much of von Schlieben."

The muscle in Hitler's jaw began twitching. His Alsatian dog, Blondi, who'd been asleep under his desk, awoke and growled irritably. "Who appointed von Schlieben to command the fortress at Cherbourg?" Hitler demanded.

"Rommel," Keitel replied.

"ROMMEL!"

"Yes, mein Fuehrer. Rommel."

"Rommel," Hitler mumbled, getting up from his desk and pacing back and forth on the rug, his hands behind his back. Rommel had been one of his favorite generals, a brilliant commander and fierce warrior in North Africa where he'd smashed numerically superior British and American forces, but then he lost the crucial battle there, and then he'd lost in Italy, and now he was losing in France. Last time Hitler saw him, Rommel had appeared demoralized and unsure of himself. He'd suggested that Hitler seek a political solution to the war, and Hitler had thrown him out of his office. I should never have made him a field marshal, Hitler thought, and I never should have permitted Goebbels to make him a national hero. Maybe I should have Rommel shot.

But he realized that if he had Rommel shot, he'd have no one better to replace him with. Huge numbers of generals had been killed on all fronts in the war so far, and more were being knocked off every day. Why, only a week ago General Erich Marcks, commander of the LXXXIV Panzer Corps, was hit by a bomb as he was leaving his command post at Saint-Lo. And besides, if Rommel was sacked, the German people wouldn't stand for it. Rommel had become an immensely popular personality, thanks to Goebbels. Maybe Goebbels ought to be sacked instead.

"May I make a suggestion, mein Fuehrer?" Keitel asked.

"What is it?" Hitler snapped.

"I studied our maps and troop dispositions before I came here," Keitel said, "and I'm afraid we can't hold Cherbourg. Therefore I suggest that we abandon the Cherbourg Peninsula and withdraw the five divisions we have there to a defensive position farther east. Then perhaps we can contain the Allied incursion, and when we build up our strength, push them back into the sea."

Hitler stopped abruptly and subjected Keitel to a

withering stare. "Withdraw?" he asked softly.

Keitel stiffened in his chair, because he knew that his Fuehrer was about to explode. "It was only a suggestion," he said weakly.

"Withdraw?" Hitler asked again.

"It was something that just came to mind on the spur of the moment," Keitel explained affably.

Hitler raised his fists over his head. "If that's what came to your mind, you mustn't have much of a mind!" he screamed. "Withdraw from Cherbourg? Have you gone mad?"

"No, mein Fuehrer."

Hitler pointed his long bony finger at him. "Cherbourg will be defended to the last man, is that clear?"

"Yes, mein Fuehrer."

"You will issue those orders to Rommel without delay!"

"Yes, mein Fuehrer."

"And you will send a personal message from me to General von Schlieben. You will tell him to conduct the battle for Cherbourg just as Gneisenau fought to defend Kolberg!"

"Yes, mein Fuehrer."

"Do you have any questions?"

"No, mein Fuehrer."

"Please be so good as to carry out your orders!"

"Yes, mein Fuehrer." Keitel leapt to his feet, gave the Hitler salute, and ran out of Hitler's office, being careful to close the door softly behind him, because his Fuehrer hated loud noises.

Hitler returned to his desk, propped up his elbows, and rested his chin on his hands. Straight ahead through the windows he could see the magnificent craggy mountains of the Alps. The walls of his office were wood-paneled, and the draperies were maroon. Covering the walls were various portraits of himself.

How can all this be happening to me? Hitler wondered gloomily. After all I've been through, after all the difficult decisions that I've made correctly, why is everything going wrong now?

And it was true, for only thirty years ago he was an unknown young artist living in a Vienna flophouse with the dregs of Europe. From that nadir of human existence he had risen against all the odds to become Fuehrer of the Third Reich and conqueror of Europe. There were those who said that he was reason incarnate, and if that were so, why was everything going wrong now? Could it all be some kind of divine test, the last one God would give him before making him ruler of the world?

Yes, Hitler thought in his madness, it must be that. I am losing now only so that I might win a great battle in the future. It became perfectly clear to him that the key to that great future was the defense of Cherbourg. If he could keep that port from the Allies, perhaps he could destroy them on their pathetic little beachhead, and then he could concentrate all his forces on the Russian Front, pushing through to the Kremlin and shooting Stalin like the mad Bolshevik dog that he was.

Hitler smiled as he contemplated the world after he defeated the Allies and the Russians. He'd design huge architectural masterpieces that would stand for tens of thousands of years to commemorate his great deeds. He'd be greater than Julius Caesar, Alexander the Great, Napoleon, and Bismarck himself.

He'd be the greatest man who ever lived.

And to achieve all that, he just had to keep the Allies out of Cherbourg.

EIGHT

The mud-spattered bullet-riddled Mercedes-Benz limousine slid to a stop in front of a huge chateau in La Roche-Guyon, and a haggard-looking Field Marshal Erwin Rommel opened the back door. He got out of the limousine and stomped through the mud to the front steps of the chateau, which he then climbed. The soldiers in front of the door presented arms and he saluted them back as one of his aides ran ahead and opened the door.

Rommel entered the vestibule of the chateau he had been using as his headquarters. He was returning to it after an exhausting and demoralizing two-day tour of the front, a tour that convinced him that the war was lost, that Germany was finished, and all he could do was slow the Allies down and make them pay the highest price possible for every inch of ground they won. The Allies would achieve victory eventually—he was convinced of that—but he'd make them remember and fear the name of Rommel forever.

Aides rushed to him from all the rooms to salute and welcome him back to La Roche-Guyon. He shook their hands and told them he was happy to see them again, and indeed he was, because he'd had a few close calls at the front. Once a squadron of fighters had broken through the cloud cover and strafed the road he was on, but he'd managed to jump out of the limousine and hide in a ditch. It was infuriating that the Allies had complete domination of the skies due to the indolence and stupidity of that fat old drug addict, Reichsmarshal Goering.

Lieutenant Steuben rushed toward him and saluted. "Sir, Field Marshal Keitel is on the phone from Berlin and wishes to speak with you!"

Rommel grunted and walked swiftly toward his office, wondering what that fool Keitel wanted now. As far as Rommel was concerned, Keitel was the foremost ass-kisser in the Reich, and much of the blame for the collapse of the German Army could be laid at the feet of Keitel, who always said yes to Hitler instead of opposing him with sound military arguments, but maybe Keitel didn't know of any sound military arguments. Maybe he'd been around Hitler too long and his brain had gone soft.

Rommel sat behind his desk and looked at the photograph of his wife and son. They were in Ulm and he hoped they were all right. He picked up the telephone and barked: "What is it?"

There was a pause at the other end, and then an edgy, irritated voice radiated out of the earpiece. "This is Field Marshal Keitel."

"I know," Rommel said. "What's on your mind?"

"I say there, Rommel. This is still the German Army and I'm still your commander. Have you forgotten how to behave to your commander?"

Rommel decided that he'd better continue playing the military game, because Keitel had the ear of Hitler, and if Keitel expressed too many adverse opinions about Rommel, it was not inconceivable that a little SS detachment might show up at La Roche-Guyon one of these days and put Rommel up against a wall. It had happened to others and Rommel had no doubt that it could happen to him too.

"I'm sorry, Herr Field Marshal," Rommel said. "I've just returned from a personal tour of the front and it was quite grueling. I almost lost my life a few times to enemy bombs and strafing attacks."

"I quite understand the pressures of your command, Herr Field Marshal. But we must all endeavor to maintain military protocol no matter what."

"You're right of course."

"I have a message for you from the Fuehrer. He asked me to call you personally and relay it to you. He considers it to be of the utmost importance to the future conduct of the war."

Rommel groaned. "I know what it is already."

"You do?" Keitel asked, startled.

"Of course," Rommel replied. "He orders me to hold fast on all fronts and to fight till the last man."

Keitel chuckled. "How cynical you've become."

"Is that the message or isn't it?"

"That's the message more or less, but it applies this time to Cherbourg."

"Cherbourg?" Rommel said. "I've written Cherbourg off long ago!"

There was silence on the other end for a few moments. Then Keitel said: "You shouldn't have done that."

"We can't possibly hold it, Keitel! We don't have the troops, and it doesn't make sense anyway. We should move all our forces back to a secure line and fight the Allies from there."

"I've already mentioned tactics like that to the Fuehrer, and he wouldn't hear of it."

"Maybe it's time something were done about our Fuehrer," Rommel hinted darkly.

"I didn't hear that!" Keitel screamed.

"Calm down," Rommel said.

"Let's get back to Cherbourg," Keitel suggested.

"By all means. Hitler wants me to hold it until the last man, isn't that correct?"

"Yes."

"Very well. You've delivered your message. Tell the Fuehrer that I will carry out his orders to the best of my ability? Is that all?"

"No," said Keitel. "I want to discuss actual tactics with you, because if Cherbourg is not defended to the last man, it will be my neck as well as yours, do you understand?"

"I understand, but I told you I'll do my best."

"According to my table of organization, you have five divisions on the Cherbourg Peninsula, isn't that correct?"

"Four," replied Rommel.

"I thought there were five."

"There were five, but now there are four."

"What happened to the other one?"

"I've pulled it back."

"You've pulled it back!"

"Correct."

"Why did you do that!"

"Because an opening appeared in the American lines, and I saw a chance to save the Seventy-Seventh Division. I ordered it to escape through the gap, and it did so, returning to our lines and capturing along the way two hundred fifty prisoners, eleven military vehicles, and thousands of meters of telephone cable. I thought it was a very adroit maneuver and I've already phoned Colonel Bacherer to congratulate him."

"You shouldn't have done that," Keitel said.

"I'm trying to save our Army," Rommel replied. "Can't you understand?"

"Hitler is going to be very angry when he finds out."

"To hell with him."

"Rommel," Keitel said wearily, "you're giving me a lot of problems."

"If you think you've got problems, you should come over here. I can't even hold together the semblance of a front line."

"Let's get back to Cherbourg, and I don't want you to interrupt me until I'm finished, is that clear?"

"Yes, sir."

"First of all, you should not have pulled out the Seventy-seventh Division without authorization from me."

"You mean I have to call you whenever I want to move a paltry division around?"

"Yes."

"Then I'll have to call you twenty-five times a day!"

"I told you not to interrupt me. To continue with what I was saying, let me remind you that Adolf Hitler, our Fuehrer, still is commander-in-chief of the Army, and he still makes the final decisions. If he wants to defend Cherbourg to the last man, all we can do is say *Heil Hitler* and carry out our orders. Is that clear?"

"Come on, Keitel," Rommel said chidingly. "We know more about war than he does. It's true that he's made a few right guesses, but he's made a great many mistakes as well, such as the decision to attack Russia before we defeated Great Britain. No, I think officers like you and I must make sensible military decisions with an eye toward defending the Fatherland and keeping the Army as strong as we can. My only regret is that I was unable to remove the other four divisions off the Cherbourg Peninsula and save them also."

"You're going to go too far someday, Rommel," Keitel warned.

"It's a little too late to worry about nonsense like that."

"Let's go back to Cherbourg. My orders to you are to defend it the last man."

"Why?" asked Rommel.

"Why? Because it's a vital port, that's why."

"Then our only hope is to destroy the port."

"That's part of the strategy, and you know it. Presumably efforts are being made to mine the harbor and blow up the docks, is that not so?"

"Yes, but it won't mean very much."

"Why won't it mean very much?"

"Because once the Americans take Cherbourg they'll clear out the mines and rebuild the docks. I predict that within a month they'll have the port functioning normally, and then we'll really be in trouble."

"That may be so," Keitel agreed, "but the main thing is to follow the Fuehrer's orders and fight to the last man."

"I disagree most respectfully, sir. The main thing is to deny use of the port to the Americans."

"How can we do that?"

"By utterly destroying it for all time."

"We don't have enough demolition charges for that."

"Oh, yes we do," Rommel said.

"We do?"

"Yes."

"Not according to my information."

"That's because you're only considering *Army* information. You perhaps are not aware that our U-boat service has used Cherbourg as a refitting station, and that there still are tons of torpedoes stored in the naval facility there. If we used those torpedoes as demolition devices, the port could be utterly destroyed to the point where the Americans would have to build an entirely new harbor, which is almost like building a whole new city, instead of merely sweeping away some minefields and rebuilding some docks."

Keitel thought for a few moments. "Are you sure that can be done?" he asked eagerly.

"I know it can," Rommel replied. "I've already discussed it with my engineers and they say if divers are used to place large quantities of explosives on the bottom of the harbor deep in the muck, they can blow the whole harbor sky-high."

"But won't the water damage the explosives so that they won't go off?"

"Does water damage torpedoes, Keitel?"

"Hmmm. Well, I suppose it's a feasible plan. How soon do you think you can get it under way."

"It's already underway. I had intended to destroy the port, and then pull all my divisions off the Cherbourg Peninsula in one mad dash through the American lines."

"No, you'll have to leave the divisions there, Rommel."

"It's a waste of four fine divisions, Keitel."

"But that's what the Fuehrer wants."

"Then that's what he'll get."

"He'll be very happy to learn about your intended destruction of the port."

"Well, I hope it works. We don't have much time, you know. The Americans are moving up the peninsula rather quickly."

"You've got to bring it off, Rommel. I'm sure you know that the Fuehrer hasn't been too happy with you lately. It's a way you can restore his confidence in you."

"I'll do my best."

"I'll see the Fuehrer right away and tell him of your plans. He's been in a bad mood lately. It might cheer him up."

"Maybe you shouldn't mention what I did with the Seventy-seventh Division."

NINE

The driver of the jeep, a young Pfc, wrestled with the steering wheel as he tried to dodge the holes. Beside him sat Mahoney, smoking a cigar and hanging onto the windshield frame. He held a carbine between his knees and his full field pack was lying in the space behind the front seats.

A battle was taking place not far away. You could see explosions and a haze of gunsmoke about 700 yards ahead in the rolling fields of the Cherbourg Peninsula. The jeep just had passed the American artillery emplacements that were bombarding the German lines, and occasionally a German shell would fall into the fields, blowing mud and sod into the air. The fields were littered with destroyed German and American tanks, some of them still smoking. Mahoney could see that this peaceful farmland had been hotly contested not very long ago.

The Pfc pulled the jeep to the side of the road and stopped. He took out a wrinkled, filthy map and squinted at it. The map was covered with pencil marks and Mahoney wondered how anybody could read it. The Pfc looked to his right and pointed in the direction of the battle.

"The Twenty-third Rangers should be just about over there," he said.

Mahoney looked in the direction of the Pfc's finger. "You're sure about that?"

"Yes, sergeant." The Pfc pointed to the map. "See?"

"I can't see a goddamn thing."

"Well, that's where they are, or at least where they were this morning."

"Why don't you drive over there and we'll see?"

"Can't do that, Sergeant. Got to bring the jeep back to headquarters."

"You're supposed to deliver me to my unit," Mahoney argued.

"That's what I've done," the Pfc said self-righteously, "but I'm not supposed to place my jeep in danger. Them's my orders."

Mahoney pointed to the field. "There's not much going on over there."

"Oh, yes there is. I'm sorry, Sergeant, but this is as far as I'm supposed to go."

Mahoney looked at him and grunted. The Pfc was a typical rear echelon soldier, scared to death of getting killed. What he needed was a few months up on the line—that'd change his whole vision of the world. It'd make him more accustomed to danger, and if he didn't get killed too soon he'd learn a lot about it. He'd find out that there were gradations of danger, and that some frontline situations are safer than sitting in the command post in the rear, because artillery shells fall quite frequently in the rear, and that's how high-ranking officers get killed.

"You can look mean all you want to, Sergeant,"

the Pfc said nervously, "but I don't have to go up there and I'm not gonna."

Mahoney slapped him easily on the shoulder. "It's okay, kid. Take it easy."

Mahoney got out of the jeep and rapped his knuckles on the top of his steel helmet. He pulled his full field pack out of the jeep and ran his arms through the straps. His blanket and tenthalf were tied to the top of the pack and bent down its sides like a horseshoe. When it got dark he'd find some other asshole and button both their tenthalfs together. If Cranepool still was alive he'd buddy up with him.

Mahoney took his carbine in his left hand and waved it to the Pfc. "Thanks for the lift, kid."

"Good luck, Sarge."

"You too. Watch your step on the way back."

The Pfc nodded and shifted into reverse. He backed up and around in the round until he was pointed more or less in the direction from which they'd come. Then he shifted into gear, tugged the wheel around, and rumbled off.

Mahoney stood on the shoulder of the road and watched him go, thinking, here I am again. Puffing his cigar, he slung his carbine over his shoulder and trudged into the field, heading for the front lines. He knew that a German artillery shell might land on his head at any moment, and that scared him a little, but he knew that the odds were against it. A stray German machine-gun bullet could blow through his heart, but the odds were against that, too. Mahoney had learned long ago that in combat you had to play the odds, otherwise you'd be scared shitless all the time.

He shifted the weight of his pack and puffed his cigar, still moving toward the front lines. He passed a destroyed German tank lying on its side and emitting faint streams of gray smoke at the sky. Nearing it, he could feel the intense heat from the charred metal. He peered through the big jagged hole in the front deck of the tank and saw a mass of blood and bones inside, smelling like cooked guts.

Pulling his head away, he spit onto the ground and took a deep draught of fresh air. Then he continued his solitary march toward the front, thinking that he'd do anything rather than serve in a tank. He thought tank duty was the most dangerous and horrible in the entire Army, because you had to sit inside a big slow target and you couldn't run and hide anywhere. The odds were high that you'd be roasted alive or blown into unrecognizable red pulp. Mahoney couldn't understand men who volunteered for the tank corps. They had to be out of their fucking minds.

An Army truck appeared over the crest of a hill straight ahead and came toward Mahoney. He watched it approach and it passed by only a few yards away from him. Turning to look at it, he saw two soldiers sitting in back underneath the canvas.

"Here you go, Sarge!" one of them shouted in a southern accent, tossing a package out the back.

Mahoney knew what it was before it hit the ground: Assault Rations. Evidently the truck had been passing them around at the front lines. He stopped and took off his pack, laying it on the ground and opening it up. He stuffed the canned food inside, put the pack of cigarettes in his shirt pocket, and thought he'd eat the candy bar on his way to the front. Putting his arms through the straps again, he put his cigar butt in the pocket with the cigarette pack, peeled the wrapper off the candy bar, and bit half of it away, munching like a bull as he walked to the front.

He looked at his watch, and it was four o'clock in the afternoon. He'd awakened that morning at a repple depple (replacement depot) in England. Yesterday morning he'd awakened at the hospital in Southwick. He'd spent the night before that saying goodbye to Shirley in the hotel where they'd first made love. She cried while he was screwing her and he'd felt like crying too. The sex was pretty good, although it was strange and bittersweet and drenched in her tears. She said she'd never forget him and he told her she'd better if she ever hoped to get any peace of mind. Perhaps she was so good in bed because she was so tormented by guilt. Lovely little thing, though. Very nice blowjobs. If the world had been different he would have asked her to marry him, but the world wasn't different, she was a lieutenant and he was a dogface, and she was supposed to marry her Navy pilot if he ever came back alive.

Probably neither of us will come back alive, Mahoney thought as he plodded over the field. The sound of battle was closer and he could see explosions and flashes of small arms fire in woods 400 yards to his front. That's where the Americans were, and he assumed that the Germans were a few hundred yards beyond them in the same woods. He could see tanks rumbling around and shooting at each other in the distance behind the woods, and there were a number of hills back there that he figured were heavily fortified by the Germans.

"Oh, this fucking war," he growled as he tucked his head down a few inches. He didn't know when he'd screw a woman again or when he'd eat a hot meal. He might even be killed in the next five minutes. The Germans back in those hills could see him through binoculars and could call an artillery strike in on him if they wanted to be shitty about it. It would be a shameful waste of ammunition, but once he'd seen an American artillery sergeant blast away a cow like that just for the hell of it.

It was strange to have passed so quickly from London to the front lines. He didn't know whether he was dreaming that he was here or had dreamed that he'd been there. He knew that his instincts were off and he wasn't in very good physical shape because he'd been lying in the hospital bed for most of his days and screwing Shirley for most of his nights. He hadn't even had time to shoot craps in the latrine, and only had forty-two dollars in his shirt pocket. Maybe when they got to Cherbourg he could do a little black market thing with the connivance of a mess sergeant. He'd arranged deals like that in North Africa and Italy, and had made a lot of money, but he'd spent it all on booze and whores.

He finished the candy bar and relit the stub of his cigar. Here I go, he thought, leaving the field and entering the woods. Drops of rainwater fell from the branches onto his helmet, making an inordinately loud sound to his ears. The woods smelled like swampwater and gunpowder. He heard the *whump-*

whump-whump of mortars being fired and headed in that direction, keeping his head low. He passed shell craters with shattered trees lying all around them. Other trees had bullet holes in them. The fight was taking place a few hundred yards in front of him. Bullets and shrapnel whistled past him sporadically, and he moved forward with his head nearly as low as his knees.

Finally he came to the mortar squad. A private was arming the mortar rounds, a Pfc was dropping them down the tube, and a corporal made adjustments in the sights. Another private was opening a crate of fresh mortar rounds, and the crew was in a foxhole a few feet deep. Mahoney slid into the hole with them and the private opening the crate went for his carbine.

"Cool your motor," Mahoney said, getting the drop on him with his own carbine.

The others turned around, saw that he was in the same Army they were in, and relaxed.

"Keep firing," Mahoney said to the corporal. "Don't stop just because you got a visitor."

"You heard him," the corporal said to the Pfc who was supposed to be dropping the mortar rounds into the tube.

The Pfc dropped a round into the tube, and it went *whump* as it came back out. It moved quickly but Mahoney could see it make a high arc into the sky, and then come down hopefully on the head of some Kraut.

"Where are the Twenty-Third Rangers?" Mahoney asked.

"The Twenty-Third Rangers?" the corporal

replied. "Never heard of them."

"They're supposed to be right around here," Mahoney said.

"Search me."

"What outfit are you in?"

"Fourth Division, Fifteenth Regiment."

"Do you know where you are on the line?"

"Whataya mean?"

"Are you on the right flank, the left flank, or kind of in the middle?"

"How the fuck am I supposed to know?" the corporal said.

Mahoney puffed his cigar and hooded his eyes. "You're doing a great job, kid. They're all talking about you."

"Yeah?" the corporal said, like a wise guy. "What are they saying?"

"They're saying that you're a fucking asshole. So long, and it might be a good idea if you found out where in the fuck you are."

Mahoney climbed out of the hole and moved to his left, staying in a low crouch. There probably weren't any Germans around to worry about, but there were lots of stray bullets and shrapnel. He was getting close to the fighting and could feel the special excitement that went along with it. His glands started to pump out adrenalin, making him tense and sharp-eyed. He liked the feeling, and a lot of front-line soldiers liked it so much that they volunteered to stay close to the enemy, because you never feel so alive as when you're close to getting your head blown off.

Mahoney pushed a branch to the side with his carbine, but it snapped back and hit him in the face. He touched his finger to his cheek and it came away with blood. He'd just got there and already he was bleeding. That was a bad omen, and Mahoney became superstitious when he was at the front. He started believing in fate and all that shit, but he couldn't help it when, for instance, he'd be sitting in a foxhole for a few hours, and then after leaving it to take a quick shit, it would be hit with a German artillery shell.

He thought about the corporal in the mortar squad he'd just left. Clowns like that had caused him to volunteer for the Rangers. He'd realized very early in the war that the regular line infantry divisions were filled with guys like that corporal who didn't know shit from Shinola. They walked around in a daze, following orders on the most simplistic level, making the absolute minimum of effort, and as a result, were not reliable in tight situations. Mahoney realized that if an enemy was trying to kill him, he'd better surround himself with men on whom he could rely, men who brought some professionalism into the front lines with them, men who knew what in the fuck they were doing.

He chose the Rangers because he figured they were the Army's elite. A Ranger theoretically was supposed to know how to do anything. He could jump out of planes like paratroopers. He was skilled with knife, garrote, or his plain bare hands. He was trained to fire, maintain, and strip down *all* of the Army's weapons. He also was trained in all the specialties of the Army, such as communications, demolition, map reading, combat engineering, and ordnance. Rangers were kept in tip-top physical condition and every day that they were in garrison they studied tactical problems so that they could command a squad, platoon, or company in every kind of action conceivable on any type of terrain imaginable.

Mahoney had been a so-so soldier in the infantry, but he really came into his own in the Rangers. The challenges of an elite unit brought out the best in him and slowly he earned his stripes, but more importantly, he proved himself in that great acid test: battle. He'd earned a reputation as a cool head and a hard charger. In Italy his platoon used to joke around and say that he was made of steel, and he actually believed this after a while, but then one day he caught that shrapnel in his gut, and he discovered that he really wasn't made of steel.

He kept moving in a southerly direction parallel to the front lines, keeping his head down and hoping that the Twenty-Third Rangers were in this part of the woods. It would be good to be back with the old crew, and he was looking forward to it. He figured that the Twenty-Third Rangers were to the American Army as the French Foreign Legion was to the French Army: a collection of crazy, violent bastards who for the most part had been the dregs of society in civilian life, but had coalesced into a crackerjack front-line fighting unit.

Through the rattle of machine-gun fire and explosion of artillery shells, he heard human voices. Stopping and peering around a tree in their direction, he saw five American soldiers crouched behind a huge boulder ten feet in diameter. One of them was turning the crank on a field telephone and the others watched him intently. Mahoney ran toward them and they all went for their guns until they realized he was a GI.

Mahoney got behind the boulder with them. The one turning the crank on the field telephone was a young captain, and he was with two lieutenants and two sergeants.

"I'm looking for the Twenty-Third Rangers," Mahoney said. "Are they around here?"

The captain pointed in the direction that Mahoney had been moving toward. "They should be about two hundred yards thataway, but if it's a war you're looking for, we've got one right here."

His statement was punctuated by the whistle of an artillery shell overhead, and they all dropped to their stomachs. The shell exploded fifty yards away, knocking down a bunch of trees.

"See what I mean?" the captain said.

"I've got to rejoin my unit, sir," Mahoney said. "Thanks for the directions."

"Keep your head down, sergeant."

"Yes, sir."

The captain got to his knees and continued cranking up his field telephone, while Mahoney moved off in the direction of the Twenty-Third Rangers.

TEN

In Cherbourg, Lieutenant Keller of the *Wehrmacht* engineers, entered the front door of a five-story apartment building and climbed the wide stairs. He was compactly built, of less than average height, and had blond hair. His back was stiff as a ramrod as he moved up the stairs, and his visored cap was cocked jauntily to the side of his head. When he reached the fourth floor he turned right down the hall and knocked on a door toward its end.

It was opened by a wraithlike young brunette who would be considered quite beautiful were it not for the fact that her nose was about a half-inch too long for her face.

"Helmut!" she said happily, holding out her arms and moving toward him.

He hugged and kissed her. "My darling Francine."

"You're late, I was beginning to think that you weren't coming."

"I've been very busy, and I can't stay long."

She wrinkled her long nose as he entered her little flat. "But I've cooked dinner!"

"I'll be able to eat a little, but then I have to get

back to work."

"What's keeping you so busy?"

"Oh, it's a long story. After I wash my hands I'll come to the table and tell you."

He skillfully threw his hat onto the rack, then ambled to the bathroom which was located in the bedroom. Francine watched him until the wall hid him from her view, then went to the stove and took the cover off the pot of pea soup that she was cooking. She wore a blue cotton dress with little red flowers imprinted on it, and a white apron that had a few food stains. Opening the oven, she looked at the chicken being kept warm in there; it was surrounded by a gravy containing sliced carrots and potatoes.

Helmut returned to the kitchen, kissed Francine again, and sat at the kitchen table, unbuttoning his tunic. "Smells good in here," he said.

"I've cooked a marvelous supper for you," she said crossly, "and you can't even sit and enjoy it."

"There's a war on, darling. Don't you know that?"

"Yes, I know it, but it's not here yet."

"It'll be here soon enough, don't worry."

Francine ladled the soup into bowls. She'd made the stock with real ham bones that Helmut had secured from his mess hall. He'd also obtained the chicken from somewhere in his Army post. There were all sorts of advantages to being the girlfriend of a German officer, and Helmut had no illusions about the motivation for Francine's professed love for him, but what he didn't know, and indeed would have been horrified to learn, was that Francine was a spy for the Free French, and reported daily to her superior officer on information she gleaned from Helmut's conversations.

Francine brought Helmut's bowl of soup to the table and set it before him. Then she got behind him, crossed her arms over his chest, and kissed his ear. "I've missed you so much," she said.

"I wonder if you'd love me if I didn't bring you chickens and ham bones."

She pouted. "I'd love you anyway, but maybe not as much as I love you now."

He laughed. "At least you're honest."

"I will never lie to you, my dear," she replied as she returned to the stove.

"Well," he said, blowing on his soup, "the war will be over someday and we'll see about that."

She ladled soup into a bowl for herself. "Sometimes I think the war never will end."

"It will, don't worry about it. We can't hold out much longer. It might even end this year."

She carried her bowl to the table and sat down. "This year, Helmut? Really?"

"I'm afraid so. I just hope I'll be alive when it's all over."

She placed her hand on his. "I'll save you, darling."

"I may need you to do just that someday."

"You can rely on me always, Helmut."

"I hope so."

He took a spoonful of soup and raised it to his lips. "Ouch!" he said, burning his tongue.

"Let it cool off."

"I don't have time."

She looked at him and smiled. "Oh, yes, you said

you'd tell me what's keeping you so busy."

He frowned. "A very big job."

"What kind of big job?"

He gazed into her eyes. "You must promise not to breathe a word of this to anyone."

"Of course I promise. Who would I tell?"

"I don't know, maybe one of those teachers you work with in school."

"I wouldn't tell them something like this."

"I know you wouldn't intentionally, but you might let something slip sometime."

"I won't let anything slip," she said annoyed that he didn't trust her completely. "Have I ever blabbed anything that you told me not to?"

"Not that I know of."

"Well?"

He blew on his spoon of soup, then put it into his mouth and swallowed it down. "It's very good."

"I'm so glad you like it, but don't change the subject."

"Oh, Francine, leave me alone, will you?"

She shot to her feet abruptly and placed her hands on her hips. "You don't trust me!"

He smiled wanly. "Oh, stop being so French, will you?"

"Well!" she said, stamping her foot. "After all we've been through together, I can see that you still don't love me and probably never will."

"I do love you, Francine. Please sit down and stop screaming. I have to leave very soon, don't spoil the few minutes I have to spend with you."

"You can leave right now for all I care!"

"Oh, you French are so emotional."

"And you Germans know nothing of love. It's true what they say: you're all made of ice."

"And fire," he said with a wink, trying to lighten the conversation.

"And distrust!" she shot back.

"I don't distrust you."

"Then why won't you tell me what you're doing? I know why you won't tell me. Because you're seeing another girl, that's why!"

He laughed. "That's funny."

"So now you're laughing at me, eh!" She threw the potholder at him, and it bounced off his head. "What's her name, tell me so that I can kill her!"

"Oh, really," Helmut said. "This is getting to be too much."

"Who is she!" Francine screamed.

"Calm down."

"I won't calm down until you tell me her name!"

He groaned. "There is no one else, Francine. I told you that I've been very busy lately, and I meant it."

"Busy doing what!"

"Sit down and relax, and I'll tell you." He looked at his watch. "And hurry up because I don't have much time."

She smoothed her hair and sat at the table. "Well?"

"We're making preparations to blow up the harbor," he said, "because the Americans will be here soon and we don't want them to use it."

She raised her eyebrows. "I thought you already were doing that."

"We are, but we're also doing something far more

damaging that will utterly demolish the harbor so that the Allies will be unable to use it for a few months, maybe longer."

"Oh, I see," she said.

"It's a very big job. I'll tell you in advance when we're going to throw the switch, so you can prepare yourself. There'll probably be quite extensive damage."

"But Helmut, what about you? Where will you be?"

"Deep underneath the fortress, my dear. We in the engineers will set off the blast from down there."

She looked at him and thought for a few moments. Then she raised her nose in the air. "I don't believe you," she said.

"You don't?"

"No, I don't."

"Why not?"

"Because where would you get all the explosives to do that kind of damage? You can't fool me, Helmut. Now I know you've got another girl. Imagine telling me a ridiculous lie like that. Why, even I know that no new supplies have come to this city for a week, ever since the Americans cut off the peninsula."

Helmut smiled. "Well, that's the tricky part," he said.

"It certainly must be," she replied coolly.

"But you see my dear, the explosives have been here all along, but in another form."

"What are you talking about, you big liar!"

"Don't you remember that U-boats used to come to Cherbourg for refitting?"

"Are you trying to say that the U-boats brought in the explosives!" she said angrily. "Even I know that U-boats can't get through that mined harbor, and moreover, everybody knows that the Allies have sunk nearly all of your damn U-boats! Tell me another one, you liar!"

"You haven't let me finish," Helmut said. "You're right, the U-boats don't come here anymore, but we still have vast stores of torpedoes and torpedoes are filled with gunpowder, understand?"

"Ah! You're taking the gunpowder from the torpedoes!"

"Not exactly. We're just burying the whole torpedoes in the muck underneath the docks and running detonation wires to them. We have a great many torpedoes here—enough to blow this harbor to kingdom come. And when the time comes, we'll also pour our remaining gasoline into the water, so that when we blow the torpedoes, flaming gasoline will explode in all directions. That ought to slow the Americans down, don't you think?"

She smiled, aware of the importance of the information she'd just obtained. "It certainly ought to," she agreed.

"Now do you believe me when I say that I don't have another girl?"

She covered his hand with hers. "I'm sorry. How could I have doubted you? But you know how emotional I can be."

He nodded as he brought a spoonful of soup to his mouth. "You French," he said.

Francine picked up her spoon and dipped it into

her bowl of soup, hoping that Helmut would leave soon, so that she could deliver the information to the *maquis* underground headquarters on the Rue Garonne.

ELEVEN

Captain Albert "Bulldog" Boynton sat cross-legged in a foxhole, eating a cold can of beans. He was commander of Easy Company, Twenty-Third Rangers, and had received his nickname because he had a pug nose, squashed face, and beady little eyes. He was a Texan, forty-five years old, had rounded shoulders and no ass, and had risen from the ranks to his present position in the officers corps of the U.S. Army.

Bullets and artillery shells whistled over his head, and explosions were now taking place all around him, but he calmly finished his beans, smacking his lips and pausing occasionally to scratch his balls. He was not unduly disturbed by being on the front lines, because he'd been a combat soldier since he was seventeen, and had fought in all the major battles of the First World War, in addition to his considerable front-line service in this new war.

Bulldog Boynton felt odd when things were too quiet and bullets and artillery shells weren't whistling over his head.

He tossed the empty can out of his foxhole and reached into his back pocket for his little flask of bourbon. Suddenly he heard the heavy clomping of running feet, and darted his hand toward the Colt .45 in his holster. Glancing over the rim of his foxhole, he saw a huge figure in an American uniform running toward him with his carbine at high port arms. The figure dodged tree stumps and boulders, jumped over bushes, and did a feet-first slide into Bulldog Boynton's foxhole.

"Master Sergeant Clarence J. Mahoney reporting for duty, sir," said the huge figure, saluting as he came to a stop with his knees touching Bulldog Boynton's.

"Well, I'll be a son-of-a-bitch," wheezed Boynton. "When in the fuck did you get back?"

"Just today," Mahoney replied with a grin. "I reported to battalion first and they told me you were over here."

Bulldog Boynton held out his hand. "Welcome home, Sergeant."

Mahoney shook it. "It's good to be back."

"This calls for a drink." Bulldog Boynton reached into his back pocket and took out his stainless steel flask of bourbon whisky. He always carried it with him and it never went empty, which was the source of much speculation and mystery in the Twenty-Third Rangers. He unscrewed the cap and passed the flask to Mahoney. "Here you go, Sergeant."

"Thank you, sir." Mahoney took the flask and poured some bourbon down his throat. It burned his innards and made him feel good. Handing the flask back to Boynton, he felt that he was back where he belonged, and everything was going to be all right.

Boynton took a healthy swig, wiped his mouth

with the back of his hand, and jammed the flask into his back pocket. "I heard you was in a hospital in England," Boynton said in his Texas drawl, "but I don't suppose it was anything serious since you're back."

"Just a little leg wound," Mahoney said.

"I got shot in the leg once," Boynton said. "It was in the battle for Soissons during the First War, which was before your time. I was a private in the Second Division then. A leg wound isn't shit, but I guess you know that." He winked at Mahoney. "You fuck any nurses?"

"One."

"Only one?"

"She was enough."

Boynton spat. "Wish somebody would shoot me in the fucking leg, so maybe I could get myself some hospital pussy."

"But what would Easy Company do without you, Bulldog?"

"Fuck Easy Company. I'm getting sick of this war. It's been raining too much."

"It'll stop."

"I'm not so sure. It's been raining ever since we hit the beach, just about."

"How's it been going except for the weather?"

"We've lost a lot of people."

"Kraut bastards."

Boynton shook his head. "Fucking mess. I guess I'll give you the second platoon."

"What happened to Hardesty?" Mahoney asked, referring to the former platoon sergeant of the second.

"He's now my first sergeant. Don't ask me where he is because I don't know."

"What happened to Cullen?" Cullen had been the former first sergeant.

"He's now the battalion sergeant major. Nowicki, who used to be sergeant major, got hit by an artillery shell while he was out in his jeep."

"No shit," Mahoney said.

"When the smoke cleared they couldn't find enough of him to put into a cigar box," Boynton said.

They thought about that for a few seconds, because the same thing could happen to them at any moment.

"Who's the platoon leader of the Second Platoon?" Mahoney asked.

"You are."

"What happened to Lieutenant Finley?"

"Dead."

"How?"

"Machine gun burst just after we hit Omaha. We've lost about forty percent of our people since then."

Mahoney scratched his cheek. "Has Corporal Cranepool ever come back?"

"Yeah, he's got one of the squads in the weapons platoon."

"Can I get him in my platoon?"

"You'll have to give up one of your squad leaders to the weapons platoon."

"That's okay by me."

"Okay, work it out with Del Bello."

"He's got the weapons platoon now?"

"Yeah."

"What happened to Rusitsky?"

"Shot through the head."

Mahoney shook his head and blew air out the corner of his mouth. "If this war keeps on, we're not gonna have anybody left."

Boynton nodded. "I know."

They looked into each other's eyes and wondered how long they'd be alive. The sound of running footsteps came from their rear. They turned toward the sound and saw a wiry little soldier with one hand on his helmet running toward them. When the soldier neared the foxhole he let out a yell and dived head first into it, landing in a heap beside Boynton and Mahoney. The soldier scrambled to his knees and saluted.

"Pfc Shapiro reporting, sir!"

Boynton looked at him with displeasure. "What the fuck do you want?"

Shapiro was a runner from battalion headquarters. "Colonel Kersey wants you to knock out the pillbox on hill four-five-one, sir."

"Oh, shit." Boynton took out a map and unfolded it. Squinting, he ran his finger over the grid lines until he found the hill. "Here it is," he said, pointing to it.

Mahoney leaned to his side and looked. Boynton turned to Shapiro.

"What do we know about the pillbox?" he asked.

"It's got an anti-tank gun and two machine guns, sir."

"Any other Krauts on the hill?"

"Don't know, sir."

Boynton sucked a tooth. "Okay, you can go."

"Colonel Kersey wants to know what time the pillbox can be expected to be knocked out, sir."

"Tell him an hour and a half."

"He'd like to be notified when the pillbox is knocked out, sir."

"I'll send a runner."

"Okay, sir. If you don't have anything else, sir, I'll get back to battalion, sir."

"I don't have anything. Shapiro."

"Thank you, sir. Goodbye, sir."

Shapiro crawled out of the foxhole, looked around, sprang to his feet, and ran back to battalion headquarters.

"Crazy little fucker, isn't he?" Boynton asked, his map on his lap.

"I don't think I ever saw him before," Mahoney said.

Boynton looked at the disappearing figure of Pfc Shapiro. "He probably won't last much longer." Boynton looked at the map and placed his finger on hill four-five-one again. "Since you just got back and you're full of piss and vinegar, why don't you take this fucking pillbox?"

"Okay."

"You should be able to do it with two squads."

"Right."

"Get going, and it's good to have you back, Mahoney."

"It's good to be back," Mahoney lied, touching a few fingers to the brim of his helmet in a kind of half-ass salute.

Boynton made a little wave in reply and reached

for his flask as Mahoney crawled out of the foxhole. He crawled forward toward the second platoon, as the ground shook with explosions and projectiles whizzed overhead. However it was only casual fire, without the intensity and drama of a full-scale battle. That would come later when he tried to take the pillbox. As he moved forward he peered through the bushes and saw that Easy Company was deployed in a reasonably straight line at the edge of the forest, and ahead were rolling fields and a river, a few hundred yards away. On the other side of the river were hills, and presumably the pillbox was on one of them, in a good spot to rake anything before it with machine-gun fire, or to knock out tanks with its big gun. If you fired artillery shells at the pillbox they'd just bounce off and explode harmlessly in the air. So you had to take it with a bunch of dogfaced soldiers, using stealth, courage, brains, and TNT.

But first he had to get his platoon organized. He came to a machine-gun emplacement, pouring bursts of bullets at the German positions across the river. Crawling into the foxhole with the machine-gunner, he asked where the second platoon was.

"Sergeant Mahoney!" said one of the Pfcs. "You're back!"

"Yeah, I'm back," replied Mahoney, who didn't even know who the Pfc was.

"Glad to see you, Sarge!" the Pfc said, holding out his big ham hand.

Mahoney shook his hand. "Thanks."

"The second platoon's over there," the Pfc said, pointing.

"Thanks again."

Mahoney crawled out of the foxhole and moved forward in the direction indicated by the Pfc. Puffs of smoke appeared on the German side of the river, where soldiers were firing at the Americans. Far in back of that pillbox the Germans must have the artillery that was shelling the American lines, but the shelling wasn't very heavy, which meant either that the Germans didn't have too many artillery pieces, or they didn't have very much ammunition.

Mahoney came to a foxhole which at first he thought was empty. Then, as he looked into it, he saw a little private lying on his back smoking a cigarette. He slid into the foxhole, and the private looked lazily at him.

"Hi," the private said.

Mahoney glowered at him, his face turning red. "What in the fuck do you think you're doing, soldier!"

The private arched his eyebrows. "Who wants to know?"

"Who wants to know!" Mahoney bellowed. He grabbed the private by the front of his shirt and held him in the air. "I want to know!"

The private turned white and his lips trembled as he looked at the master sergeant's stripes on Mahoney's arms. "Hello, Sergeant," he said weakly.

Mahoney threw the private against the wall of the foxhole. "Get your rifle, you little shit, and start shooting!"

The private fumbled with his rifle and put it against his shoulder. He clicked off the safety switch in the trigger guard and squeezed off a round. Taking aim again, he squeezed off another round. Then he turned to Mahoney and said sheepishly: "I was just taking a little break, Sarge."

"I ought to put a little break in your face, you sawed-off scumbag. What's your name?"

"Flynn."

"Where you from, Flynn?"

"New York City, Sarge."

"I thought I heard the Broadway local in your disgusting mealy-mouthed voice, Flynn. What platoon are you in?"

"The Second Platoon, Sarge." His hands trembling, Flynn squeezed off another round.

"Well whataya know about that?" Mahoney said. "I'm your new platoon sergeant, Flynn. My name's Mahoney."

Flynn turned around. "Mahoney? Are you the Sergeant Mahoney who was working behind the lines in France with Corporal Cranepool."

"Yeah."

"Oh, I heard a lot about you, Sergeant Mahoney. You're a real son-of-a-gun, they all say."

"Knock that shit off, Flynn. Who's the platoon leader here right now?"

"Sergeant Kirk."

"Go get him and bring him back here."

"Yes, Sergeant."

Flynn crawled out of the foxhole and Mahoney leaned his back against its wall, taking out a cigarette and lighting it up. He blew smoke into the air and thought that the Second Platoon must have deteriorated badly since Lieutenant Finley got hit on Omaha. Well, they were going to start shaping up starting that afternoon. He looked at his watch, and it was four-thirty. It wouldn't be dark for a few hours, which should be enough time to knock out that pillbox.

Flynn returned to the foxhole with Sergeant Kirk, a lanky redhead from Oklahoma. "Glad to have you back, Sarge," Kirk said as he slid into the foxhole.

"Wish I could say I was glad to be back," Mahoney replied. "Listen Kirk, I was just talking to the old man about you and he said to transfer you to the Weapons platoon, so you might as well get rolling over there right now and report to Sergeant Del Bello, got the picture?"

Kirk frowned, "Yes, Sergeant." He wasn't very happy about it because he was being demoted back to squad leader again, after the heady experience of commanding a platoon.

"And tell Sergeant Del Bello that the old man said to transfer Corporal Cranepool to the Second Platoon immediately and without delay, get it?"

"Got it!"

"Good. Give me your maps and shit, and get going."

Looking like he'd just lost a month's pay in a poker game, Kirk handed over his mapcase, binoculars, and other gear that went along with a platoon leader's job.

"Who's your runner?" Mahoney asked.

"Private Gomez."

Mahoney looked at Flynn. "Go get Gomez and tell him to report to me."

"Right, Sarge."

Flynn crawled out of the foxhole, and a few

minutes later Kirk departed for the weapons platoon. Mahoney puffed his cigarette and thought that if he was in garrison he'd hold a few inspections and a few hours of physical training every day to whip the platoon into shape. He'd raise hell and take names, maybe bust a few corporals and Pfcs just to wake everybody up. But there was no time for that now. He had to take that pillbox before it got dark. It would be better to sneak up on it at night and take it in the morning, but Colonel Kersey wanted it tonight. He probably didn't need it tonight, and could get it much cheaper in the morning, but orders were orders. "Oh, this fucking Army," Mahoney muttered.

Flynn returned with Gomez, who was of average build and had a brown Mexican face. He carried a bazooka and walkie-talkie in addition to his carbine. Gomez had been with the Twenty-Third Rangers since the old days in the States, and Mahoney knew who he was. Gomez had been a corporal once but had allegedly stabbed somebody in a bar. He was said to be a good man with a knife, providing he was on your side.

"Hello there, Sergeant Mahoney!" Gomez said happily. "When you get back?"

"Just now. I'm the new platoon sergeant and you're gonna be my runner, got the picture?"

"Sure, I got the picture. Hey, Sarge, when are we gonna go on pass! I ain't had a pass since I can't remember when. Hey, I need some poozy, Sarge."

"Shut up, Gomez. I'm trying to think."

"Hokay, Sarge."

Mahoney took out the map of the area and looked

at Hill 451. He probably could take the pillbox there with two squads but he'd need to have his flanks covered. He'd once heard General Patton give a speech in which he said: "We're not going to worry about our flanks, let the Germans be the ones to worry about their flanks!" But Mahoney's front-line experience told him that was bullshit. If you didn't watch your flanks your ass was grass and the Germans had the lawnmowers.

"Gomez," he said. "Give the bazooka to Flynn."

"Aw, Sarge," Flynn said. "I don't want the damn thing."

"Take it you little son-of-a-bitch and don't give me no shit."

"Aw Sarge."

Gomez handed over the bazooka and Flynn slung it around his shoulder. Mahoney wanted his runner to travel light so that he could get where he was going faster.

"You stay close to me, got it, Flynn?"

"Okay, Sarge,"

"You're gonna be my special bazooka-man, got it."

"I am?" Flynn asked, delighted.

"Yeah, but you're not going to get paid any more for it."

Flynn didn't know whether he'd been promoted or not. Mahoney told him to dig a foxhole six feet away and to remain alert. As Flynn was leaving Mahoney's foxhole, Corporal Edward Cranepool came sliding in like Ty Cobb trying to steal second base.

"Hiya, Sarge!" Cranepool said happily, smacking

Mahoney on the shoulder.

"Hello there, Cranepool," Mahoney replied. "How're you doing?"

"Oh, all right, Sarge. Gee, I was thinking that you were never going to come back."

"I'm like a bad penny, Cranepool. I always come back."

"How's your leg, Sarge?"

"Just about all better."

"You have fun in London?"

"A little. How's everything been going out here?"

"It's just one continual pile of shit, Sarge. We've been shooting and fighting day in and day out. It's not like when we were behind the lines in France."

"Yeah, well duty like that only comes along once in a lifetime." Mahoney looked at the map. "Listen, we gotta knock out this pillbox here on Hill 451, see it?"

Cranepool squinted at the map. "Yeah, I see it."

"Bulldog said to take it with two squads, but our flanks will be wide open, so we'll have to take the whole platoon. We'll have one squad on each flank and two squads will go right up the middle. Get the picture?"

"I got the picture, Sarge."

Mahoney looked at Gomez. "Go get the other squad leaders."

"Righto, Sarge."

"And keep your fucking head down."

"Yo."

Gomez crawled out of the foxhole and Mahoney and Cranepool went over the map, planning their tactics for knocking out the pillbox. Mahoney glanced at his watch and it was nearly five o'clock. He didn't have many hours left before it got dark. Gomez returned with the four squad leaders; Sergeant Franklin, Corporal Devers, Sergeant Patch, and Corporal Voukevich. Mahoney told them he was the new platoon sergeant and Cranepool was his new assistant.

"Any questions?" he asked.

None of them had any questions, so he proceeded to explain their mission to them. They'd all get into a skirmish formation with Sergeant Franklin's first squad on the left, Corporal Devers's and Sergeant Patch's squads in the center, and Corporal Voukevich's fourth squad on the right flank. Mahoney and Cranepool would be with Corporal Devers's squad. They'd jump off at five-thirty and race across the field to the river. The second and third squads would cross the river while the first and fourth squads covered them. Then the third squad would cover the second squad as it charged the pillbox, went around to the back door, and laid the TNT against the door. They'd blow the TNT, and that would be the end of the pillbox. Mahoney would radio back that the pillbox was out of action and presumably all the troops in the vicinity would advance across the river.

"Any questions?" Mahoney asked.

Nobody said anything.

"Okay," Mahoney said, "go back to your squads and get ready." He looked at his watch. "We'll jump off in about fifteen minutes. Get going, and good luck."

The squad leaders scrambled out of the foxhole,

leaving Mahoney, Cranepool, and Gomez inside. Flynn was in the foxhole a few feet away, checking the sighting mechanism of the bazooka.

"Cranepool," Mahoney said, "Go to Ordnance and get the fucking TNT."

"Hup Sarge."

Cranepool crawled out of the foxhole and Mahoney lit another cigarette. It would be his last one for a while, and he wished he had a cigar to chew on.

"Hey, Gomez, you got a cigar on you by any chance?"

"A cigar? What would I be doing with a cigar?"

"I don't know. Just thought I'd ask." Mahoney cupped his hands around his mouth. "Hey, Flynn, you got a cigar on you?"

"No, but I got the bazooka."

"You fucking asshole."

Mahoney puffed his cigarette and tried to work himself into a frame of mind to attack the pillbox. He wondered if this would be the mission from which they'd bring him back in a box. He wondered what Shirley was doing just then, and a homesick ache for her developed in his stomach. Three nights ago he was screwing her in a funky old hotel, and now he was sitting in the dirt with Private Gomez.

"Don't think too much, Sarge," Gomez said with narrowed eyes. "It's gonna give you a headache."

"I'm going to give *you* a headache if you don't keep your mouth shut and speak only when you're spoken to."

"Aw c'mon, Sarge, don't get chickenshit with me, okay?"

Mahoney looked coldly at Gomez. "Gomez, you and I are gonna have a little talk when this pillbox shit is over with."

"Good. I like talks," Gomez said.

"You won't like this one, fuckhead."

Cranepool slid into the foxhole, a young dynamo of energy and enthusiasm, which was why Mahoney liked him so much. He held up a big bulging haversack. "I got the TNT, Sarge."

"Good going." Mahoney looked at his watch; it was five twenty-five. "We've got five minutes to go," he said. "Get ready."

"I stay ready, Sarge."

Mahoney looked at Gomez. "Call Bulldog and tell him we're jumping off in five minutes."

"Hokey-doke, Sarge."

Gomez pressed the button on the walkie-talkie and mumbled into the mouthpiece. Mahoney took a final drag on his cigarette, and tossed it over his shoulder. He unstrapped his canteen from his waist and took a swig of water, wishing it was beer. Returning the canteen to its case, he checked his carbine and worked the bolt a few times. The adrenalin was starting to run in his body, making him a little crazy. Kill or be killed, he thought. That's what it's all about.

He looked at his watch, and the minute hand crept closer to five thirty in the afternoon. A light rain was falling and Mahoney wondered who was going to die today. The law of averages said that at least one person would get hit, and it most probably would be the person who wasn't watching his ass. The front was no place for dreamers.

The minute hand touched five thirty, and it was

time to go. Mahoney came up out of the foxhole with his right fist in the air, the signal for infantry attack.

"Follow me!" he screamed.

He jumped out of the foxhole and ran through the woods toward the field. He saw his platoon emerge from their holes like a bunch of rats and join him in a wide skirmish line. He looked to his right and saw Cranepool with his carbine at high port arms, leaping over a bush and screaming a battle cry. The sight of that enthusiastic, bloodthirsty young trooper invigorated Mahoney, who gave a war whoop and blasted through a bush to the open field.

The woods around them erupted with the sound of machine gun and small arms fire, as the rest of the Easy Company provided cover for the Second Platoon in its 300 yard dash in the open to the bank of the river. Gomez yelled something in Spanish and on the right flank there came a rebel yell. The platoon advanced in a long wave across the open field, and ahead of them they saw explosions on the other side of the river where the Easy Company weapons platoon was dropping in mortar rounds.

Mahoney pumped his legs and held his elbows wide. "YAHHHHHHHH!" he screamed. "BLOOD AND GUTS!"

"BLOOD AND GUTS!" echoed Cranepool, and then the rest of the platoon said it: "BLOOD AND GUTS!"

Their feet sounded like the hooves of horses as they thundered across the field. They leapt over shell craters and the bodies of dead Germans, as enemy machine guns chattered on the other side of the river, and the horrible whistling of German artillery shells started coming in on them.

Mahoney knew that German artillery was zeroed in on that field, and so did the men of the Second Platoon. They had dreaded this moment and now it had come. German artillery shells exploded in their midst, but they kept on moving, because to stop and hide was to die.

"FASTER!" Mahoney yelled. "WE'RE ALMOST THERE!"

But they weren't almost there; they had 200 yards to go, and these 200 yards would be the toughest of all. An artillery shell landed on the right flank of their line, blowing three soldiers into the air. Machine-gun bullets brought down two on the left flank, and then Flynn went down screaming, trying to cover his face with his hands, a face that was spurting blood and brains, a face whose skull was flying into the air.

"KEEP MOVING!" Mahoney bellowed.

The German shells kept coming in, and Mahoney could smell the acrid gunpowder. A burst went off twenty feet in front of him and he ran through the falling hail of muck. Huge explosions rent the air on the opposite bank of the river; old Bulldog must be calling in heavy artillery from the Division. The German machine-gun fire diminished but the German artillery shells kept landing. They blanketed the entire field, but the Second Platoon was a thin green line moving steadily through it, and there were very few direct hits.

The river bank came up fast, and it had a little dirt embankment at its edge.

"TAKE COVER!" Mahoney screamed.

The Second Platoon approached the river bank and dived behind the embankment. It was only two feet high but it was the distance between life and death. Mahoney landed against the embankment with his head and left shoulder, and as he hit and smelled the damp earth he thought of Shirley in the London hotel room. He looked to his left and right and saw his men adjusting their steel helmets and burrowing into the crannies of the embankment.

Mahoney wished he had a cigar. His heart was pumping loudly and his hands tingled with excitement. But this was no time to rest; you had to keep the momentum going.

"Gomez!" Mahoney yelled.

"I'm right here," said a voice beside him.

"Call Bulldog and tell him to stop the artillery."

"You got it."

"Cranepool!"

"I'm here, Sarge."

Mahoney looked at Cranepool, who was third man down the line on his left. "You still got the TNT?"

"Hup, Sarge."

"Stay close to me." Mahoney cupped his hands around his mouth. "When I give the word, we're going across the river!" he yelled. The first and fourth squads will cover the second and third! Then, when we get over there, the third will cover the second, which will make the actual assault on the pillbox! Any questions?"

Nobody said anything. Mahoney jumped up and held his carbine high in the air. "UP AND AT

'EM!" he screamed.

The Second Platoon came up from behind the embankment, jumped over it, and scrambled over its side into the river. Mahoney led the way, holding his carbine high in the air, taking huge strides across the fast-moving river, which deepened beneath his feet and soon came up to his chest.

"KEEP MOVING!" he screamed, looking ahead to the enemy shore, where American artillery shells were still falling. Mahoney hoped the artillery would stop pretty soon, because the Second Platoon would be there in a couple more minutes. He heard the steady rifle fire of the first and fourth squads, plus the chatter of their BARs. Ahead were bushes and skinny little trees. Somewhere among them were Germans in trenches, and the background was the grassy hill with the pillbox on top. "KEEP MOVING."

The river was cold and made him shiver. It tugged at his clothes and tried to drag him downstream. German bullets blipped into the water around him, and he heard a shout from his left, turning to see a GI's head go under, the victim of a direct hit from a German rifle. "FORWARD!" Mahoney stumbled on a rock and nearly went under himself, but regained his footing and kept moving. He saw Cranepool holding his bag of TNT high in the air and Gomez holding up the walkie-talkie. The Second Platoon climbed up the far side of the river bed, the water dropping to their waists and then their thighs. "DOUBLE-TIME!" Mahoney shouted.

They ran out of the river and the artillery bombardment of the German position stopped abruptly. All Mahoney could hear now was the steady fire of his first and fourth squads, pouring hot lead into the German position from the extreme flanks. "MARCHING FIRE!" he screamed.

They tucked their rifles against their hips or into their shoulders and marched forward in a skirmish line, firing a round every two or three steps. Advancing steadily toward the German trench emplacements, their deadly fire kept the heads of the Germans down, and then, when the Germans realized they had to fight or die, they raised their heads and got them shot off.

In front of Mahoney, three German soldiers jumped out of their hole and charged, firing their rifles from their hips. Mahoney shot one through the stomach, Gomez got one in the balls, and the third lunged at Mahoney with his rifle and bayonet, but Mahoney parried it neatly, smashing the German upside his head with his rifle butt, and the German sagged to the side, his jaw broken and blood foaming out of his mouth. He fell to the ground and Mahoney ran him through with his bayonet, placed his big foot on the German's chest, and yanked the bayonet out.

The second and third squads overran the German position and Mahoney ordered them to take cover. They dived into the German foxholes next to dead German soldiers and reloaded their rifles. The machine guns in the pillbox up the hill were raking them back and forth, having claimed a few victims during the river crossing, and several more in the assault on the German trenches.

Mahoney ground his teeth together and looked at

his watch. It only had been five minutes since his platoon left the Easy Company position, but it seemed like hours. He took out a cigarette and lit it up, inhaling the aromatic smoke into his lungs.

"GOMEZ!" he yelled.

"Hair I am, Sarge."

"Call the first and fourth squads and tell them to direct their fire into the pillbox!"

"Hokay Sarge."

Mahoney took a few more puffs of the cigarette. He looked at the dead German in the foxhole with him. The German had received a bullet on his nose, and Mahoney could see his brains through the opening. Mahoney flashed on an image of himself similarly hit, and shuddered.

"SERGEANT PATCH!" Mahoney shrieked.

"I'm here, Sarge," Patch said in his lazy Tennessee drawl.

"Open fire on the pillbox!"

"Yo."

Mahoney heard Patch give the orders to his squad, and then the steady fire began. Then Mahoney called out to the two BAR men in the second squad, telling them to stay behind with the third squad and pour lead into the little openings in the pillbox. Mahoney took another drag on his cigarette and positioned it at the corner of his mouth. He'd like to stay and rest for a few minutes, but in an attack you had to keep pushing forward and not give the enemy a chance to do much planning.

"Where are you Cranepool?" he shouted into the evening breeze.

"Over here, Sarge."

Mahoney peered over the top of the trench and looked at the pillbox. Its machine guns weren't firing anymore because the German soldiers inside didn't dare look out their peepholes, for a hail of lead was zinging through them. Mahoney remembered the pep talk he'd heard General Patton give in North Africa. Patton had said: "Grab 'em by the nose and kick 'em in the pants." That meant that an attacking army must pin the enemy down in front with one bunch of soldiers while attacking in the rear with another bunch. Now Mahoney had the pillbox pinned down, and all that remained was to move his second squad behind it for the final kick in the pants.

"SECOND SQUAD, FOLLOW ME!" he yelled, charging out of the trench.

He veered left, jumping over smoking shell craters and the dead bodies of German soldiers. He saw arms, legs, and heads separated from their torsos, but stuff like that didn't affect him anymore. Glancing over his shoulder, he saw the second squad behind him, Cranepool carrying the TNT and Gomez with the walkie-talkie. It still was raining lightly and blood mixed with the water running in little gullies. The Fourth Division artillery had given the Germans a terrific pounding, but it had paid off. Mahoney had lost few men and now was moving steadily and resolutely toward his final objective.

The pillbox was only 200 yards away, sitting ominously on top of the gently-sloping hill. Mahoney and the second squad circled the hill and then ran up its back, where the pillbox had no peepholes or armaments. The cigarette hung from the corner of Mahoney's mouth and his heart chugged in his chest as he led the squad up the hill. They were almost there now. The Germans could come out the back door of their pillbox and fight them, but Mahoney had never seen that happen before and doubted whether it would now. He wondered what the Germans inside were thinking. Were they scared or did they think they were safe? Mahoney thought that pillboxes were even more dangerous to be in than tanks, because at least tanks could move. Pillboxes just sat there, big white targets, and it wasn't that hard to knock them out if you knew what you were doing.

The second squad knew what it was doing, and Mahoney didn't have to say a word. They rushed toward the rear of the pillbox and stopped twenty yards away, getting onto their stomachs and holding their rifles on the door in case the Germans decided to come out. Cranepool ran forward alone, his bag of TNT in his hand, crouched over and ready for anything. Cranepool dashed toward the door, laid the bag of TNT against it, opened the flap, and tripped the detonator. Then he sped away, his back arched and head low, diving head first into a little hollow on the side of the hill.

Mahoney rested his nose on the ground, putting his steel helmet between him and the TNT. He waited patiently, chewing the butt of his cigarette, it wouldn't be long now, and BAARRROOOOMM-MMM!

The TNT went off exploding the pillbox's back door to tiny splinters. A huge puff of smoke rose from the door and blossomed into the air. The men of the second squad had their hand grenades ready, and threw them into the opening where the door had been. The countryside resounded with the multiple explosions, and more smoke issued from the pillbox.

"UP AND AT 'EM!" Mahoney yelled.

They got to their feet and charged the rear door of the pillbox. When only ten feet away, Mahoney held out his hand, and they moved in slowly. Mahoney was the first one at the door, and peeped inside cautiously. It smelled like gunsmoke and cooked guts, and the curved walls had a red slick on them. The machine guns and artillery piece were twisted from the heat, and there wasn't much left of the German soldiers. The only way to tell how many of them there had been was to count the mangled helmets. There were six of them. Tough shit for you, Mahoney thought.

He turned to Gomez. "Call the C.O. and tell him we've got the pillbox."

"Hokey-dokey."

"The rest of you guys take a break, but be ready for a counterattack."

They deployed themselves on the military crest of the hill, the part that gave them full view of the rest of the hill and the fields and woods in the distance. Mahoney sauntered to the front of the pillbox and looked down at the river and American positions on the other side. Like ants, the American troops were moving forward, now that the pillbox had been knocked out. They'd keep moving forward until something else stopped them, and then they'd go over it or under it or just plain smash through it, as they made their way up the peninsula.

Mahoney returned to his skirmish line and dropped down beside Gomez. "You raise Bulldog?" he asked.

"Sure did."

Mahoney turned to Cranepool. "Good work," he said, slapping Cranepool on the shoulder.

Cranepool fidgeted around and blushed like a little boy. Mahoney took his binoculars out of the case and looked ahead. He saw tank tracks but no tanks, and foxholes but no Germans. Evidently the Krauts were retreating to a new defensive line, and the soldiers in and around the pillbox had been left behind to slow down the American advance. Well, they hadn't slowed it down for long.

Mahoney raised his binoculars, and the countryside rushed past his eyes. In the distance, through the rain and mist, he thought he could see the ocean, and it looked as though a city was out there, nestled comfortably in a bay.

"I think I see a city," Mahoney said, chewing the butt of his cigarette.

"If you do," Cranepool replied, "it must be Cherbourg."

TWELVE

Lieutenant General Lightning Joe Collins sat behind a folding desk in a wall tent 100 yards from a road that led to Cherbourg. It was evening, the sun having set in the west only a half-hour ago. Lightning Joe was studying reports from his front lines, piecing them together in his mind so he could have an idea of the gains his VII Corps had made that day. If he kept his present pace, he was sure he could be at the gates of Cherbourg in two days, and he thought he could reduce the garrison there in less than a week.

There was a commotion in front of the tent, and Lightning Joe looked up. One of the soldiers on guard stepped into the tent and saluted. "Colonel Kersey is here to see you, sir."

"Send him right in."

"Yes, sir."

The soldier went outside, and a few seconds later Colonel Richard Kersey, the commanding officer of the Twenty-Third Rangers, entered the tent, his helmet under his arm. He advanced smartly to the front of Lightning Joe's desk and threw a snappy salute.

"Colonel Kersey reporting, sir."

"Have a seat, Kersey."

Kersey sat on a rickety wooden chair and placed his helmet on the vacant chair beside him. He was tall and lean, with blond hair and a three-inch scar on his cheek. A graduate of West Point, he was known throughout VII Corps as a fighting fool. He watched Lightning Joe shuffle papers on his desk, evidently looking for a particular one of them. Lightning Joe's eyeglasses glinted in the light of the kerosene lamp on his desk, and the flickering flame made eerie shadows in the corners of the tent. Kersey thought Lightning Joe looked more like a college professor than the hard-charging combat general that he was.

"Ah, here we are," Lightning Joe said, pulling some papers and a map out of his pile. "I've got a special assignment for you, Kersey."

Kersey leaned forward in his chair. "What is it, sir?"

"Come around here, would you?"

"Yes, sir."

Kersey walked around to the rear of the desk as Lightning Joe spread out the map. Kersey looked over Lightning Joe's shoulder and could see that the map was of a city. At the corner of the map was scale information and the word *Cherbourg*.

Lightning Joe looked sideways at Bulldog. "A serious problem has come up, Bulldog, and you'll have to take care of it for me."

"What is it, sir?"

"We've just received word from the *maquis* in Cherbourg that the Germans there have devised a monstrous plan for destroying the harbor." Lightning Joe pointed to the harbor of Cherbourg. "We knew that they had the harbor mined and that they're demolishing the docks, but we expected that and were ready for it. Now, however, the *maquis* tells us that the Germans are going to do much more serious damage than we'd imagined. Bend over here, will you?"

Kersey bent over the map, and Lightning Joe pointed to the system of docks that extended into the harbor. "Like I said, we expected damage to the docks," Lightning Joe began, "but we figured it all could be repaired within a reasonable amount of time—a few weeks or a month, let's say. But those sneaky damned Germans are burying a network of torpedoes in the bay underneath the docks and the warehouse areas. When those torpedoes go off, they'll not simply damage the docks but also utterly destroy the pilings underneath them and leave nothing left for us but a bay full of rubble. We had intended to have those pilings for our own use, and it's essential that we have them to build our own docking area upon, so that we can start pouring reinforcements and supplies into France. But now it appears that we won't be able to use the harbor for several months. It's a very serious situation, as you can see, Kersey."

Kersey considered the problem. "Maybe if we push hard we can take Cherbourg before the Germans finish their torpedo job."

Lightning Joe shook his head. "It's too late for that, I'm afraid. They've just about got it finished. When our troops get into the city, the Krauts will throw the switch. I understand that they've even got networks of torpedoes in the sewer system of the entire waterfront area, so it'll really be one helluva mess. They'll also pour gasoline around, so there'll be a terrific incendiary problem. What I want you to do is select as many men as you think you need and send them into Cherbourg as a special commando unit to stop the Germans from throwing that switch. Somehow they'll have to break through enemy lines and infiltrate the city in disguise. I honestly don't know how they're going to do it, but they'll have to do it anyway."

Kersey squared his shoulders. "If it can be done, we'll do it, sir."

"Good man. I knew you'd say that."

Kersey bent over the map. "Do we know where that switch is?"

"Yes," Lightning Joe said, pointing to a section of the map. "It's in the Cherbourg fortress, right here. See it?"

Kersey squinted at the map. "Yes, sir."

"The garrison there is commanded by Lieutenant General Wilhelm von Schlieben. We understand that the switch is in a special control room adjacent to his conference room, which is next to his office."

"That's going to be a tough nut to crack, sir."

Lightning Joe looked up at him. "But it's got to be cracked anyway. The Seventh Corps is cut off from the the rest of the Army right now, and the only outfit I've got for this type of assignment is the Twenty-Third Rangers. I spoke to General Bradley about the matter and he recommended your outfit because you've got some men in it who can speak

German and French, and who've already worked behind enemy lines."

Kersey nodded. "That's true."

Lightning Joe handed Colonel Kersey some papers. "Here's the map and your complete orders. The address of the *maquis* headquarters in Cherbourg is in there. Your men probably will want to check with them as soon as they get into the city. Any questions?"

"No, sir."

"Then you might as well get going. You have a lot to do."

"Yes, sir."

Kersey marched in front of Lightning Joe's desk and saluted, and Lightning Joe saluted back. Kersey did an about-face and stomped out of the tent. He walked through the mud outside and climbed into his jeep. His driver started up the engine, and the jeep sped away from VII Corps Headquarters.

THIRTEEN

Mahoney and Cranepool slept fitfully in their pup tent pitched beside the German pillbox they'd taken before sundown. They'd had a supper of cold Assault Rations and then wrapped themselves in their blankets and gone to sleep. They expected to attack or be attacked early in the morning, and wanted to be well rested. Other pup tents were pitched around them on the hill and down its sides. The company perimeter was patrolled by guards, but Mahoney and Cranepool didn't pull guard duty because they were NCOs. It was still drizzling, making a steady hissing sound on their tent, but they couldn't hear it. Cranepool dreamed of the family hog farm back in Iowa, and Mahoney was dreaming of Shirley the nurse.

Suddenly the tent flap was flung open and Bulldog Boynton came crawling in. "Get up and piss!" Boynton shouted. "The world's on fire!"

Mahoney and Cranepool leapt out of their blankets and went for their guns.

"It's only me, you assholes," Bulldog Boynton said, chuckling.

"What's up?" Mahoney asked.

"Colonel Kersey is here. He wants to talk to both of you."

"What about?"

"A little job that Lightning Joe wants us to do."

"What kind of little job?"

"You'll find out at the meeting. It'll be held at my command-post tent in two minutes. You'd better be there before I get back. And be ready to move out after the meeting."

"Move out where?"

"You'll find out at the meeting."

Boynton backed up through the tent flaps and disappeared into the night. Mahoney and Cranepool unwound themselves from their blankets and put on their combat boots.

"If Kersey's here, it must be something important," Cranepool said as he tied up his laces.

"Must be," Mahoney agreed, putting on his steel helmet.

They crawled out of the pup tent and made their way down the hill to the command-post tent, which was pitched between the foot of the hill and the river. The battleground still smelled of rotting corpses but soldiers had to get used to that on the front lines. Even though the German bodies had been buried by now, there was a finger lying behind a bush here, and an ear lying behind a rock there, and it didn't take much to stink up an area.

They entered the command-post tent and saw Colonel Kersey bending over the map table. Mahoney and Cranepool saluted him, and he saluted back. Then he invited them to come to the map table. He was smiling and had a gleam in his eye;

Mahoney always had the impression that Colonel Kersey loved war and that it was a big game to him, but a lot of officers were that way.

"The others will be here shortly," Kersey said in his crisp, hearty voice, leaning over the map table again. He looked at a few details of the map, and Mahoney saw that it was of Cherbourg. Then Kersey straightened up again and looked at Mahoney's stripes. "You must be Sergeant Mahoney," he said.

"Yes, sir."

"Is that Corporal Cranepool?"

"It is, sir."

Kersey smiled. "I've heard a lot of good things about you two. You did a very good job here in France, I understand."

"Thank you, sir," Mahoney and Cranepool said in unison.

"You're both fluent in French and German, I'm told."

Mahoney cleared his throat. "I'm fluent in both French and German, sir. Cranepool here's just fluent in French."

"That ought to do, I imagine."

Bulldog Boynton returned to the command-post tent with ten men. Mahoney knew all of them personally or by reputation, and knew that they were probably the best men in the company. Private Gomez was among them, as was Sergeant Patch of the third squad in Mahoney's platoon. They all saluted Colonel Kersey, who asked their names and shook their hands. Then he told them to gather around the map table, and proceeded to describe the Cherbourg situation.

The men listened grimly as they realized the nature of the mission to which they were being assigned. Colonel Kersey was a patrician from Maine, and his calm, dignified way of speaking stood out in stark contrast to the dangers he was describing.

"You'll all proceed as follows," Colonel Kersey said. "After this meeting you'll exchange your uniforms for ordinary French civilian clothes. Then you'll split up into small groups and proceed to Cherbourg. Once there you will rendezvous in the Fleur-de-Lis-Cafe on Rue Garonne, which is the headquarters for the local *maquis* organization. Captain Boynton will be in command of the operation, and Master Sergeant Mahoney will be second in command. You will reconnoiter the fortress that the Germans are using for their headquarters, and will break into it. I don't know exactly how, but there has to be a way and you've got to find it. Once inside, you must make your way to the control room and destroy the apparatus that will detonate the torpedoes. Then you must secure yourselves in the room and hold out until the Seventh Corps arrives and takes the fortress. Any questions so far?"

Nobody raised his hand.

"Good," said Colonel Kersey. "All right, let's bring something into the open right now. This is going to be an extremely dangerous mission and the chances of survival aren't especially good. Yet the mission is crucial to the further conduct of this war. If you're successful, you will save thousands and maybe even hundreds of thousands of lives. But I can't order you to go on a mission of this nature. You must volunteer for it. Therefore, if any of you don't wish to go on this mission, please step forward and leave the tent. The rest of us will understand, because a mission of this nature requires a degree of gallantry that is far above the ordinary call of duty. Anybody wish to leave?"

Nobody moved a muscle, although Mahoney figured every one of them would want to run out of that tent. He thought that the mission was suicide and probably impossible to carry out. Yet any man who left the tent would be branded a coward and a scumbag, and the word would spread throughout the Twenty-Third Rangers. The man would be treated like shit for the rest of his military career. Colonel Kersey knew that, and that was the reason he didn't speak to each man individually, providing the chance to bug out legitimately. He spoke to them collectively to make sure none of them would dare. So now it appeared as though they all had volunteered, although each of them would rather be back in his pup tent, dreaming of Mom's apple pie and the girls they'd left behind.

"Good," said Colonel Kersey with a smile, holding his hands behind his waist. "Superior."

Mahoney looked at Cranepool, and Cranepool looked at Mahoney. Their faces betrayed no expression, but their eyes said that the shit really was going to hit the fan this time.

Colonel Kersey walked down the rank of soldiers, shaking hands with each of them and wishing them luck. Lastly he came to Bulldog Boynton, and shook his hand firmly.

"Good luck, Bulldog," Kersey said.

"Thank you, sir."

"I know you can do it."

"We'll do our best, sir."

"Your best should be better than anything the Germans can do."

"Yes, sir."

"When do you think you'll be ready to jump off?"

"As soon as the clothes get here."

"They should be here within the hour."

"We'll leave fifteen minutes after that."

"Carry on, Captain Boynton."

"Yes, sir."

Bulldog saluted Colonel Kersey, and Colonel Kersey returned the salute. Then Colonel Kersey made a smart face and marched out of the tent. The soldiers stood at attention as they heard a jeep's engine start up outside the tent. The jeep shifted into gear and rolled away.

"At ease," Bulldog said.

The soldiers in the tent went limp.

"Come on over to the map," Bulldog said. "I want each one of you to memorize every detail on it, because you don't want to get caught carrying a map with you, got it?"

They crowded around the map and worked to memorize it although they'd just been awakened after sleeping for only a few hours, and they'd spent the previous day fighting for their lives. Mahoney didn't like the looks of the mission. He thought about maybe going AWOL in Cherbourg, and then when the American troops showed up, he'd simply say that he'd been captured and just escaped. It wouldn't be hard to do, and it'd be safer than trying to break into that fortress with eleven other assholes.

There was just one problem. Colonel Kersey had said that thousands and maybe hundreds of thousands of American lives would be saved if the mission was a success. Would it be worth risking his life to save those other Americans? Mahoney didn't know yet. He decided to make up his mind once he got to Cherbourg, if he ever made it that far.

"Anybody got any questions?" Bulldog Boynton asked.

Corporal Dill from the Third Platoon snorted. "This mission is for shit," he said.

"I know it's for shit, but we've got to do it," Boynton snapped. "Anybody got anything intelligent to say?"

Nobody opened his mouth.

Boynton looked around at them. "I don't like this any better than you do, but it's got to be done. Okay, I'll break you down into teams, and like Colonel Kersey said, we'll split up and rendezvous at the Fleur-de-Lis Cafe on Rue Garonne." He pointed his finger to the map. "That's right here."

They all looked at the location of the cafe, and then Boynton started pairing them off. Finally he came to Mahoney and Cranepool.

"I'm going with you two," he said. "We'll comprise the command section, understand?"

"I understand," Mahoney said, wondering how he was going to shake Boynton when it was time to go AWOL in Cherbourg.

FOURTEEN

It was three o'clock in the morning. Mahoney, Cranepool, and Bulldog Boynton walked down a deserted country road toward the city of Cherbourg. The rain had stopped but the road wasn't paved and had become a sea of mud. Every time they brought their feet down they went in up to their ankles, but all were wearing combat boots underneath their French civilian clothes. They could hear fierce fighting not far away, because elements of the VII Corps had launched a night attack against the Germans and were making good progress.

Mahoney, Cranepool, and Bulldog Boynton were on the right flank of the battle line. Their first big job would be to break through the fighting and get behind German lines. It would be an extremely dangerous procedure, but they couldn't be parachuted in because the Germans had been pushed back to a small area and there were no desolate places left to drop thirteen American Rangers. It would have been possible to leave them behind enemy lines via a submarine, but it would take days to effect the liaison with the Navy and make all the arrangements, and there wasn't enough time. So the thirteen Rangers had to go in on foot and hope for the best.

Mahoney smoked a cigarette and was disgruntled as he trudged through the mud. He was wearing dark slacks, a blue jacket with the collar up, and a gray cap with a peak in front. Cranepool had on a suit with shirt and tie, plus a natty wide-brimmed fedora. Bulldog Boynton wore a raincoat too long for him, and a black beret. We look like three shitheels, Mahoney thought. If the Germans see us they'll throw us right in the clink.

Each of them was armed with a Colt .45, and each had hand grenades in their pockets. Before leaving the Twenty-Third Rangers, they'd decided they'd rather be armed and take the chance of being searched, than be unarmed and take the chance of being shot without having the chance to fight back.

They heard rumbling behind them, and turned around. Coming up the road was a column of tanks and armored personnel carriers, headed for the front. The three Rangers got out of the road and let the column pass, and Mahoney wished he were one of the soldiers in that column, because the soldiers were on an ordinary reasonable mission, and not a suicide mission.

"Wonder what they're doing here?" Boynton asked after the column had passed.

"They must be on their way to Cherbourg," Mahoney replied.

"I know, but I didn't think there'd be much fighting on this end of the line."

"Guess there will be."

Cranepool cleared his throat, preparing to throw

in his two cents. "Maybe they're trying to break through in this sector."

Bulldog Boynton looked disgustedly at him. "With only one armored column?"

"Well," Cranepool said, "the German line is supposed to be stretched awfully thin in this sector. That's why we're going through here, right?"

"It's probably just doing a little reconnaissance," Mahoney said. "Or it might be here to slow down the Germans if they try a surprise attack through this flank. Who in the fuck cares what they're doing here anyway? It doesn't mean shit to us."

Boynton looked at Mahoney. "You sound like you got a bug up your ass."

"I'm sick of this fucking Army, Boynton."

"Who isn't?"

"I think when this war is over, I'm getting out."

"You couldn't make it on the outside, Mahoney. You've found a home in the Army."

"Fuck the Army. I've had it. As soon as I can, I'm getting out."

Cranepool cleared his throat again, because he wanted to participate in the conversation and show that he was an adult soldier too. "I'm gonna put in for Officer Candidate School as soon as I have a chance."

"You are?" Mahoney asked.

"That's right."

"It'll be a sorry day for this Army when kids like you become officers."

"What do you mean by that?"

"I mean you're just a fucking kid and you're too young to be an officer."

"Lieutenant Russo's an officer, and he's only two years older than me."

"Yeah, and I've never seen a worse asshole in my life, except for Colonel Kersey. Those sons-of-bitches are just playing at war, while guys like us have to fight it."

Bulldog Boynton reached into his raincoat pocket and took out his flask. "I think Cranepool would make a fine officer in a few years," he said, unscrewing the cap.

"A few years?" Cranepool asked. "Why so long? Why not now?"

"You need more experience."

"I got more experience than Lieutenant Russo!"

"I know that."

"Well, if he can be an officer, why can't I?"

Boynton took a swig of bourbon and looked sideways at Cranepool. "I shouldn't tell you this, Cranepool, but you ought to know it. The officers we're getting these days aren't worth a fuck. They're training 'em too fast and filling them full of useless bullshit. But if you want to go to OCS, I'll sign the papers when we get back. Okay?"

"That'd be swell, sir."

Mahoney harumphed. "Swell for who? It certainly won't be swell for the guys who have to serve under you."

"You're wrong, Sarge," Cranepool said. "I've been an enlisted man myself so I'll know how to treat enlisted men. You might even serve under me, someday. Won't that be a laugh?"

"I don't think I'll be laughing very much," Mahoney said.

Boynton snorted. "Oh, it might be pretty damned funny, you might be surprised."

"Maybe you're right," Mahoney said. He looked at Cranepool. "You'd better stop dreaming about being an officer and keep your mind on what's going on right now, got it?"

"Hup, Sarge."

They continued walking down the lonely country road. After a while they saw the tracks of the armored column veer off into a field toward the center of Cherbourg. Mahoney wondered if the column had been lost or if it was on some kind of complicated tricky maneuver devised by a general who had his head up his ass. Mahoney had a deep and powerful loathing for high-ranking officers, and did not want young Cranepool to turn out that way, because he had the makings in him of a good NCO.

The din of battle was intense toward their left, but straight ahead there wasn't anything going on. If the Germans had more men and tanks they could scoot through here and envelop the Americans, but they didn't have more men and tanks. They were outnumbered and slowly being whipped. They couldn't escape in this direction because they were too heavily engaged in the center of the line. The VII Corps would stay on their asses and mash them into the mud.

The road entered some woods. Mahoney could smell salt air and realized that Cherbourg and the ocean couldn't be very far away. He lit another cigarette and decided it would be his last one, because they were getting close to the enemy lines. Boynton took out his flask and had another swig of bourbon. Cranepool looked at the patches of starry clouds visible through the clouds and wondered what it was like to be a pilot in the Air Corps.

"HALT!" said a voice in front of them.

The three Rangers halted.

"Who goes there!" asked the voice, which was coming from behind some trees.

"Captain Boynton of the Twenty-Third Rangers and two of my men!"

"Advance to be recognized!"

Boynton, Mahoney and Cranepool looked at each other, then shuffled toward the direction of the voice.

"Halt!" said the voice.

The three Rangers halted.

"Betty," said the voice, giving the first half of the night's password.

"Grable," replied Bulldog Boynton.

"Pass on," said the soldier, who came from behind the tree, grinning proudly because he'd done the whole thing right. Another soldier came from behind another tree, also quite pleased with the performance.

Bulldog Boynton walked up to them. "How far away are the Germans supposed to be?"

"Not far," said the soldier.

"How far's *not far* supposed to be?"

"Couple of miles I reckon. How come you're dressed in civilian clothes, sir, if you don't mind me askin'."

"I mind," Boynton said gruffly. "Return to your post."

"Yes, sir."

The three Rangers continued to walk down the road. They passed the pup tents and trenches of the American soldiers who were supposed to hold the road in case of an enemy attack. Some of the soldiers were manning machine-gun nests and anti-tank guns. It wasn't much of a defense but probably all that was required in view of the circumstances.

They passed through the American defenses and entered no-man's-land. It was peaceful and quiet, and the countryside smelled like an ordinary summer night after a heavy rainfall. On either side of the road were rolling fields punctuated by small islands of forests.

"I think it's time we got off the road," Boynton said.

He led them onto the shoulder on the right side of the road, and then into the grassy field. It was like stepping through a big wet sponge, but Mahoney's feet had been wet for hours now. Sooner or later he'd have to find dry socks and put them on, otherwise he'd get the dreaded trenchfoot, which immobilized so many soldiers.

They moved across the field, hugged the edge of a wooded area, and then made their way across another field. Boynton was in the center, six feet from Mahoney and Cranepool. Boynton took a swig of bourbon and Mahoney wished he could smoke a cigarette. Cranepool thought how nice it would be to fly a nice dry airplane above the battlefield, shoot down a few German Messerschmitts, and then land in a field somewhere far behind the lines, where there were clean beds, PXs, and places where you could meet girls.

The sound of a loud metallic *clank* issued from a wooded area straight ahead, and they all dropped to their stomachs. The filthy water in the field seeped through their clothing, and Mahoney cursed under his breath. They heard another metallic sound, and then some laughter. A man called someone else a fool in German.

"Krauts," Mahoney said softly.

"I wonder how many?" Boynton asked.

"There's only one way to find out. One of us will have to go and have a look-see."

"You just volunteered. Go ahead."

"Oh, fuck," Mahoney mumbled as he commenced crawling across the field. He had 75 yards to go before he hit the woods, and was glad it was a dark and moonless night, otherwise his silhouette might show up against the grass, and he might become the target for a German sharpshooter. Using his knees and elbows for locomotion, he made his way across the wet grass. He cursed the Army, the war, Bulldog Boynton, and Colonel Kersey. He wished he had a cigar and he'd like to go to sleep in a warm dry bed. He wondered what Shirley was doing just then, and hoped she wasn't screwing another guy.

He reached the edge of the woods and lay still in the darkness under some bushes. The Germans were talking in low voices about the war and what it would take to make them surrender. Mahoney knew that German defenses were light at this point in the line, and wouldn't be surprised if these Germans were the only ones in the area. But there was only one way to find that out. He'd have to crawl closer and see.

Slowly and silently, he crawled into the woods, pausing every few feet to listen to the Germans. They didn't appear to be aware of his presence, so he continued forward, afraid to breathe too heavily for fear that they'd hear him. It was slow going, but it was better to be slow than dead. Finally he parted a few clumps of leaves in front of his eyes and saw in the darkness a huge ominous-looking tank parked in a clearing, and beside it were three German soldiers, talking and eating food out of cans. They didn't even have a guard posted, or did they? Surely they must have someone looking out for them. But where was he? Mahoney couldn't see or hear him. He could wait until the three Germans said something to him and he responded, but that might take more time than he had to spend. He decided to return to Captain Boynton and tell him what he'd seen. Let old Bulldog make the decision—he was the senior man on the mission.

Mahoney turned around carefully. He crawled out of the woods even more slowly than he'd crawled in, taking it an inch at a time. At the edge of the woods he rested for a few minutes, then crawled into the field again, knowing he'd be an easy target for that guard if the moon was out, but the moon wasn't out, thank God.

A half-hour had passed between the time he'd left Bulldog Boynton and the time he returned.

"What in the fuck took you so long?" Bulldog asked as Mahoney crept to within whispering range of Boynton and Cranepool.

"There's a tank in there with three German soldiers having dinner," Mahoney replied, "plus I think they have a guard out but I didn't see him."

"What kind of tank?"

"I don't know, I couldn't see too clearly."

"You see anything else?"

"If I did I would have told you. There aren't supposed to be very many Krauts in this area so I wouldn't be surprised if that tank's the only thing around."

"Hmmm," Boynton said. "I guess we'll have to go around them. He pointed to the right of the clearing. "I guess that way."

"Hey," Cranepool said, "why don't we steal the tank?"

Boynton scowled at him, "Steal the tank?"

"It'll be a lot easier going in a tank," Cranepool said. "The Krauts'll think we're one of them."

"You know," Mahoney said, "I think the kid's got something there, because if we go around the tank we'll probably bump into another German troop unit sooner or later, but if we're in the tank, nobody will know it's us."

Boynton shrugged. "A tank is an awfully big and slow target, Mahoney."

"Listen Boynton," Mahoney said, "nobody hates tanks more than me. I'd rather be anything than a tanker, but this is different. We've got to get to Cherbourg and it'll be easier in a tank. The Krauts will never suspect we're inside."

"Maybe not," Boynton said, "but do we know how to drive a tank?"

"I do," Cranepool said.

"You do?"

"Yes, sir."

"How come?"

"I fooled around with a few of them when I was in Italy."

"The kid's very good with machinery," Mahoney said. "He can drive anything."

Boynton thought for a few moments. "Okay, I guess we'll get us a tank. I suppose the best way is to circle around and take them from behind, right?"

"That's right, and we've got to be especially careful of that guard, wherever he is."

Boynton pulled out his Colt .45. "We'd better check our weapons now, because we'll make too much noise once we're in those woods."

They took out their .45s and made sure they were loaded and ready to go. Then they began crawling through the field to the right side of the small wooded area, moving noiselessly, spaced six feet apart with Boynton in the middle and slightly ahead of them. They rounded the side of the woods, crawled to the back, and on a signal from Boynton, moved into the woods. Slowly, the anxiety building within them, they crawled closer to the tank and the Germans. Finally, they saw the hulk of the tank, a black mechanical monster silhouetted against the gray sky. The German tankers sat beside it, talking in low voices. Occasionally one of them would laugh.

Boynton motioned with his hand for Mahoney and Cranepool to come closer. They did, and he whispered: "When we get within about ten feet of them, we'll charge. Cranepool and I will handle the three beside the tank and Mahoney will take care of the guard. Any questions?"

Nobody said anything.

"Let's go."

They crawled forward again, being especially careful not to make any noise. Mahoney's knee came to rest on a twig, and it cracked loudly.

"*Was war den das!*" a German exclaimed.

"GET 'EM!" said Bulldog Boynton.

They leapt to their feet and charged the Germans, firing their Colt .45s as they went. The Germans went for their submachine guns, but they didn't have a chance. Boynton shot one in the chest, pivoted quickly, and got another in the face. Cranepool pumped two fast rounds into the lungs of the third German, and Mahoney dashed to the far side of the clearing, ready to catch the guard. He held his Colt .45 in both hands for steadier aim. The guard came meekly through the bushes, his hands up. "I surrender!" he screamed.

Mahoney shot him between the eyes. The .45 slug made a little hole going in, but tore away the entire back of the German's skull on its way out. The German dropped to his knees, a surprised look on his face. Then his eyes glazed over and he plopped forward. Mahoney looked down at him, saw the brains and skull bones. Sometimes you can't take prisoners, and this was one of those times.

Mahoney picked up the German's submachine gun and returned to the clearing. The other three Germans were sprawled all around, covering the ground with their blood. They had been having a friendly little bullshit session and now they all were dead.

Boynton worked the bolt of the submachine gun he'd picked up. "Cranepool, get in that fucking thing and see if you can start it up."

"Yes, sir."

Cranepool jumped onto the rear deck of the tank and advanced toward the main hatch. He climbed down the ladder into the bowels of the tank, and it smelled like warm engine oil. It was a Mark IV Panzer tank and he'd been in one before. He lit a match and found the switch beside the control panel, turning on the inside night lights. Sitting in the pilot's chair, he pushed the lever that turned on the engine's electrical system, then pressed the button that sent energy to the starting motor. The tank motor turned and the diesel engines kicked in. He looked through the slits in front of him and could see the woods. Two big levers came out of the floor in front of him. One engaged the right tread and the other the left tread. If both of them were pushed forward, the tank would move ahead in a straight line.

Boynton and Mahoney came down the ladder. "I see you got the thing going," Boynton said.

"There's nothing to it," Cranepool replied nonchalantly.

"The sooner we get out of here the better," Boynton said. "Mahoney, you man the cannon, and I'll take one of these damned machine guns."

Mahoney pulled shut the hatch over his head and sat behind the cannon. Artillery shells were piled neatly in racks beside him. He looked through the sighting device and saw the woods in front of him calibrated in degrees.

They put on headsets so they could talk with each other above the roar of the engine. Cranepool pushed the left lever forward, and the tank turned around. When it was painted in the direction he wanted to go, he pushed the other lever forward. The treads gripped the ground and the tank moved out, rumbling across the woods, rocking and rolling around. Cranepool looked at the gas gauge and it told him he had half a tank left, but he didn't know what that meant in miles. The American Sherman tank got four gallons to the mile, and he thought this tank probably would burn gas at approximately the same rate.

The tank rolled out of the woods and across the field, churning up mud and grass. Cranepool steered in the direction of Cherbourg, hoping he could find a road soon. The tank went up and down hills, and around the islands of trees. The heat from the engine filled the tiny compartment, and they started to sweat. Mahoney took off his jacket and unbuttoned his shirt. He took a cigarette out and lit it up. His watch said it was five o'clock in the morning. Soon it would be light, but Cherbourg couldn't be very far away.

Finally they came to a narrow little road. Boynton told Cranepool to stop the tank so he could go topside and take a look. Cranepool brought the iron contraption to a halt and Boynton went up the ladder. He opened the hatch and emerged into the cool night air. He took a deep breath and looked around, listening to the sounds of battle which were now extremely close, probably not more than a few miles away.

Mahoney poked his head up through the hatch. "What's going on out here?"

"Cherbourg's somewhere over there," Boynton

said, pointing to shellbursts on the horizon.

Mahoney looked. "We should be there before long."

"That means we'll be running into Germans before long, too."

"We'll just keep on going. Fuck 'em."

"That's what I like about you, Mahoney. You don't give a shit."

"Don't be so sure about that," Mahoney said, getting down into the tank again.

Boynton followed him down and got into the seat behind one of the machine guns. "Move it out, Cranepool."

"Which way, sir?"

"The way to Cherbourg."

"But I meant how did you want me to get there?"

"You're the driver; you tell me!"

"Yes, sir."

Cranepool thought that if he was going to become an officer someday, he'd better learn how to take responsibility and make fast decisions on the spot. Pushing forward both of the control levers, the tank began moving down the road again, but the road didn't appear to be moving in the direction of Cherbourg. Maybe it was going to some goofy little fishing town or resort. Since there was no road visible that went to Cherbourg, Cranepool decided to make his own road. He tugged the left lever back, slowing the left treads of the tank. The right treads pushed the tank around in the direction of Cherbourg and then Cranepool pushed the left lever forward again.

The tank moved off the road and into a field,

rocking back and forth. Mahoney held onto his seat and decided it was time to use the straps and tie himself in.

"Where the fuck you going!" Boynton bellowed.

"To Cherbourg, sir!"

Boynton grumbled as he strapped himself to his seat. Cranepool was already strapped in. He was thinking how wonderful it would be if he could own a tank like this in Iowa and be able to drive around and scare the shit out of everybody. If he ever had any ornery neighbors he'd just go over and drive through their house.

He drove around an island of trees, and on the other side of it saw a house. The tank passed the house and came to a road that was covered with truck and tank tracks, and appeared to go toward Cherbourg. He got on the road and drove toward the city. Soon he came to an intersection, and decided to go left. He rolled along for a while longer, came to another intersection, and took a right. The houses were closer together now, and there were shell craters in the road and on the lawns of the houses. He passed a house that had been hit by a bomb, and then noticed a column of soldiers up ahead.

"Soldiers up ahead!" Cranepool said.

Boynton looked through the slits on top of the machine gun. He estimated about two companies of soldiers. "Just keep going and don't stop for anything."

"Yes, sir."

Behind the cannon, Mahoney was becoming a little claustrophobic. It was hot in the confined space and his cigarette smoke wasn't helping any. He wondered what would happen if somebody got wise and fired an anti-tank gun at the tank. Shivering, he saw himself roasting alive, his blood bubbling under his skin, his nose melting and his brain exploding.

"Captain Boynton," he said, "maybe it's time to stop this tank and get the fuck out of it."

"What the hell for? It sure beats walking."

"But we're already in Cherbourg almost. Somebody might notice us."

"They'll notice us quicker if we're outside and moving on foot. I thought you're the one who wanted to steal the tank in the first place."

"That was Cranepool." Mahoney stomped out one cigarette on the floor and reached for another.

"But you backed him up on it," Bulldog Boynton said. "Shut up and keep your eyes peeled, and for Christ's sake stop smoking. My eyes are watering enough as it is."

"Yes, sir," Mahoney mumbled, putting the cigarette back into his pack. He decided that he didn't like to go out on operations with an officer. He liked to be in charge himself. Maybe he should go to OCS with Cranepool and become an officer too.

He looked through the sighting mechanism of the cannon and could see Cherbourg. He could even make out the spires of churches and windows in the big buildings. It was dawn and the city smoked and festered in a gray haze. Shells were falling on it, but not in any great number. The heavy shelling was back down the peninsula, where the American VII Corps was mangling the Germans and pushing them back.

The tank came to an intersection and had to stop for a tank battalion moving south down the peninsula. The Germans must be sending in their Panzer reserves, Mahoney thought. They must be in a bad way. The tank battalion passed without incident, followed by three companies of soldiers in columns of twos. The soldiers trudged along with their heads down, probably half asleep. They slogged through the mud on their way to the front and none of them wondered about the lone tank sitting patiently on the east side of the intersection.

The soldiers cleared the intersection and Cranepool pushed both levers forward. The tank shuddered and moved ahead, crossing the intersection and heading toward Cherbourg. They came to a river fifty yards wide; a bridge spanned it. Cranepool crossed the bridge and entered the city limits of Cherbourg.

"I think we're here," Boynton said. "Find a quiet street someplace and drive onto it so we can get out of this fucking thing."

"Yes, sir."

Cranepool took his first left to get off the main street he was on. He was nervous now because he knew the city was a German stronghold. Looking through the turret, he saw that the streets were deserted, and that made sense to him. Most of the German soldiers would be at the front or on their way there, and the citizens of Cherbourg probably were in their cellars or down in the sewers, praying for the end of the war.

"Listen," Cranepool said. "I can see in front of me but I can't see to the side unless I turn the turret around, and that might not be a good idea. Why don't one of you two go up and see what's out there?"

"I'll go," said Mahoney, anxious for a breath of fresh air.

"I'm closer, I'll go," Boynton declared.

Boynton went up the ladder and turned the little wheel in the hatch. He pushed the hatch open and peeked outside. The only living creature he could see was an alley cat cowering beside the drainpipe of a building. The tank was headed down a side street and there were other lesser streets running down it.

"Move ahead," Boynton called down to Cranepool. "I'll tell you when to turn left."

"Yes, sir."

Cranepool pushed the levers forward and the big tank rolled on. As it approached the first intersection, Boynton told him to turn right. Cranepool pulled back on the right lever and the tank rumbled around the corner. He straightened the tank out and rolled down the center of the street.

"Stop about halfway down."

"Yes, sir."

Boynton retreated into the body of the tank and closed the hatch above him. Now he had a decision to make, and wasn't sure of what to do.

"Hey, Mahoney," he said, "do you think we should just abandon the tank or blow it up."

"Blow it up," Mahoney said without hesitation.

"But we might kill some civilians."

"If we don't blow it up, this tank might wind up killing some Americans."

"You rig the demolition."

"Yes, sir."

Mahoney took the artillery shells out of their racks and laid them on the floor of the tank, where they made a large messy pile.

"Okay, let's get out," Mahoney said. "When you're clear of the tank, run like a son of a bitch."

Boynton climbed the ladder and peeked out of the hatch. There wasn't a soul in sight. "Let's go!" he said.

He pulled himself out of the tank, jumped from the deck, and ran toward an alley. Cranepool was next, bounding out of the tank like a jungle cat, and following Boynton in the dash toward the alley. Mahoney was last and he paused in the tank's hatch. He took a hand grenade out of his pocket, pulled the pin, and placed it between his legs in such a way that the lever wouldn't spring open. Then he took out another hand grenade and pulled the pin. He dropped both hand grenades into the tank, where they landed on top of the artillery shells. Now he had four to six seconds to get away. He jumped off the tank and ran toward a telephone pole, diving behind it and hugging the sidewalk.

The tank exploded violently, shooting shards of steel and red bolts of fire in all directions. The concussion caved in the front of the old apartment building next to the tank, and that brought the roof crashing down through a few of the floors. The street was filled with dust and smoke, and Mahoney thought it was time to get the hell out of there. He jumped up and ran into the alley where Boynton and Cranepool were.

"Nice work," Boynton said.

"Yeah," agreed Cranepool, his eyes glittering with excitement.

"Let's get out of here," Mahoney said.

The narrow dank alley led to another street, and they walked quickly to it, peering around the corner to make certain there was nobody on the street, and then stepping onto it like three ordinary civilians.

They made their way through the early morning streets, heading toward the Fleur-de-Lis Cafe on Rue Garonne. Day was dawning on Cherbourg, but clouds covered the sky and made the city look dark and glum. They passed buildings gutted by direct hits from bombs or artillery shells, and some buildings had only one or two walls standing. There was no civilian traffic on the streets and only occasionally would they see a German kubelwagen or truck. On the wide Rue Marceau, the colonnades of trees wore lush bonnets of green leaves, and Mahoney thought that Cherbourg must have been a beautiful city before the war, but in a few days when the VII Corps got closer, there might not be very much left of it.

On the Rue Garonne they passed a housewife wearing a kerchief on her head and carrying an empty market basket. An old man came out of a door, stretching and looking fearfully at the three men walking toward him. A stray dog was shitting in the gutter. Cherbourg was waking up.

They found the Fleur-de-Lis Cafe; it had a little sign in front and three steps leading down from the sidewalk to a door. Descending the steps, they tried the door, but it was locked. Mahoney knocked on it, and no one responded.

"Try it again," Boynton said.

Mahoney knocked harder, hoping someone would answer because he didn't feel like hanging around the streets of Cherbourg for a few hours. The Krauts would be out in full force pretty soon.

The door was opened by a stout man with drooping walrus mustaches, wearing a filthy apron. "We're closed," he said.

"Rabouilleuse," said Mahoney, which was the password Colonel Kersey had told them to use. It was the French word for *lamb*.

"Come in quickly," said the Frenchman.

They ducked into the door, and he slammed it behind him, flipping the latches. "My name is Lousteau," he said.

Mahoney, Boynton, and Cranepool introduced themselves, glancing around the small dark room filled with tables that had chairs around them. Burnt-out candles were in holders on the tables, along with ashtrays and a few dirty glasses. Paintings of the harbor and fishing-boat scenes were on the walls.

"Are we the first ones here?" Boynton asked.

"Yes. Come with me, please."

He led them through the back door into a kitchen, and then down a flight of stairs to a dark corridor. They entered a room and Lousteau lit a candle on a big round table.

"I'll get you something to eat," Lousteau said. "You must be hungry."

"We certainly are," Boynton said.

Lousteau left the room. Mahoney took out a cigarette and lit it up. He thought that the room with its table and chairs was a good set-up for a poker game. The three of them sat silently, for they were tired after being up for most of the night. Mahoney's mouth tasted like shit and there was a dull ache in his stomach. He looked at Boynton, whose bulldog jowls appeared to be hanging even lower than usual. Cranepool was most awake, he was field-stripping his Colt .45 on the table and wiping the parts with his handkerchief. The kid's really a good soldier, Mahoney thought. That's what I should be doing. But Mahoney didn't feel like cleaning his .45. It might be dirty, but he knew it still could fire.

Lousteau returned with bread, cheese, and coffee that was mostly chicory. The three Rangers dined hungrily, not saying a word, while Lousteau watched them through heavy-lidded eyes and smoked a cigarette.

"You probably would like to sleep," he said when they were finished.

"Maybe we should speak to the person in charge here first," Boynton said.

"He's still sleeping," Lousteau replied. "He was out all night and probably will be up around noon. You can see him then, and he will show you whatever you want to see."

Lousteau led them into the corridor again and down another flight of stairs to the subbasement. Cots were jammed in side by side around the furnace and coal bin.

"This is the best we could do," Lousteau said.

Boynton assured him that the accommodations were fine. Lousteau wished them a good night, although it was six-thirty in the morning, and left the subbasement room. Without a word to each other, Boynton, Mahoney, and Cranepool dropped onto the cots and fell asleep.

FIFTEEN

Mahoney fell into a deep black sleep devoid of dreams. Shells and bombs landed on Cherbourg with increasing frequency, but he didn't hear them. The troops of General Lightning Joe Collins' VII Corps advanced steadily, pushing back the exhausted and hungry German soldiers toward the city limits of Cherbourg. The American armored divisions tore huge holes in the German lines, and the Germans fought back as best they could with dwindling ammunition and supplies. It was clear to all that the fate of Cherbourg would be decided within the next few days.

During the course of the morning, Lousteau brought Private Gomez and Buck Sergeant George Newell to the furnace room, where both promptly dropped off to sleep. At two in the afternoon, Lousteau came in again and woke up Boynton.

"Our commander is here, and would like to speak with you," Lousteau said.

Boynton raised his head from the pillow and saw that two more bodies were on the cots. Lousteau told him they'd arrived a short while ago. Boynton got up and looked at the two newcomers to see who they were. Then he woke up Mahoney and Cranepool and told them to come with him to the meeting with the Frenchman.

Mahoney rolled out of bed, and his head felt like it was filled with cement. He reached for a cigarette and looked at Cranepool, who was tousle-haired and sleepy-eyed, lacing up his combat boots. The three pulled themselves together and followed Lousteau upstairs to the room with the round table and chairs.

They entered the room and two Frenchmen were sitting at the table, eating bread and cheese and drinking wine. Lousteau made introductions, and the Frenchmen were named Carpentier and Soulanges. Carpentier was the commander, a burly man with a barrel chest; he hadn't shaved for several days. Soulanges was his right-hand man, of average height and build, quite handsome and unshaven also. The rangers sat down and were invited to share the food and wine.

"What would you like to do first?" Carpentier asked in French, gnawing a crust of bread.

Boynton's French was limited, so Mahoney answered: "I guess we should see the fortress, so we can try to figure a way to break in."

Carpentier looked at Soulanges and smiled sardonically. Then he turned to Mahoney again. "You'll never break into the fortress."

"We'll decide that after we see it."

"If you've got any sense, you'll agree with me. I'm afraid that there's no way to stop the Germans from destroying this harbor."

"Do you know if they have their torpedoes all in place yet?"

"We know that they do. They'll set them off when American troops are near the harbor."

"Well," Boynton said. "There must be some way to stop them."

"No, I don't think there is," Carpentier replied. "The control room is in the fortress, and it would take at least two regiments to storm the fortress. Entrances and exits are carefully guarded, with numerous checkpoints inside. I think it's impossible."

"Nothing is impossible," Cranepool said.

"Well, you Americans are a very optimistic people. It will be interesting to see whether or not you can get in. I hope you prove me wrong, because I was born and raised in Cherbourg, and I would hate to see it destroyed."

After the meal, Carpentier took Boynton and Mahoney to the fortress. They passed large numbers of German troops; shells were falling with greater frequency than in the morning. Soon they came to the waterfront, where gulls skipped over the waves and the smell of salt hung heavily in the moist air.

"There it is," Carpentier said, pointing to a tall, sprawling yellow stone structure a few blocks from the bay. It looked medieval and impregnable, with walls that were stripped bare of vines and too high to climb.

Carpentier took them closer to the fortress. There was a huge metal gate in front, and while they were there it opened to admit a few marching platoons of German soldiers. Mahoney and the others walked around it, and at the rear was another gate, also of steel. Mahoney estimated that it would take a lot of explosives to rip through the gate, and even if they got through, they'd probably be shot down soon thereafter. Armed soldiers could be seen atop the walls of the fortress and in the turrets.

Mahoney thought the only way to get in would be to masquerade as German soldiers and march up to the gate, requesting entrance. The *maquis* had spies and presumably could find out the procedure for gaining entrance. But once inside they'd have to gain entrance to the room where the controls for the torpedo net were located. Mahoney had serious doubts that he and the others could get through. Maybe the time had come for him to go AWOL in Cherbourg, but how could he get away from Bulldog Boynton?

Boynton scratched his grizzled jowl and looked glumly at the fortress. "It's going to be a tough nut to crack," he said to Mahoney.

"I think it's just about impossible."

"Tell your friend there that we want to go back to the cafe and have a planning session."

Mahoney told Carpentier, and they returned to the cafe. When they arrived in the basement room, three other Frenchmen were there, listening to a BBC news broadcast in French. The announcer was saying that General Montgomery had made no progress in his efforts to take Caen. Cranepool had gone back to bed, and the other two Americans were still sleeping. Mahoney wondered if the others had been captured or killed.

Carpentier told the other Frenchmen to leave, and they took their radio with them. Boynton, Mahoney, and Carpentier sat at the table, and Boynton wanted

Mahoney to ask Carpentier how they would fare if they somehow got into the fortress through one of the gates. Mahoney asked Carpentier, who replied that the fortress was the headquarters of Lieutenant-General Carl Wilhelm von Schlieben, and it would be very difficult to get through the gates. If someone was fortunate enough to get in, he'd enter a courtyard that led to several doors and passageways. These also were guarded, and another check would be made of identification papers. At each checkpoint, the papers would be checked more carefully, and Carpentier thought it was impossible to get to the office next to von Schlieben's with false identification and stolen uniforms. The security was too tight.

Mahoney conveyed this information back to Boynton, who took a swig from his hip flask and then passed it to Carpentier, who brought the metal bottle to his lips and had a taste, made a face, and handed it to Mahoney, who had a swallow, warming up his innards.

The flask came back to Boynton, who took another drink and placed it on the table. "What do you think?" he asked Mahoney.

"I think we should forget about the whole thing," Mahoney replied. "There's no way we can carry out this mission. We should just relax until the Army takes the city, and then we'll go back to the Twenty-Third Rangers."

"No," Boynton said. "We've got our orders and we've got to carry them out."

"How?" Mahoney asked.

"I don't know, but we'll have to think of something."

"When you come up with it, let me know," Mahoney said. He turned to Carpentier and asked in French. "Is there anywhere around here that I can take a bath?"

"Upstairs, but you won't be able to heat up any water because the gas mains have been closed down. By the way, what decision has your captain made about the torpedoes?"

"He hasn't made one yet. Where's the bathtub?"

"I'll have someone take you to one."

Carpentier went out into the hall and called Lousteau. The fat old waiter came down the stairs and Carpentier told him to take Mahoney to one of the rooms upstairs so Mahoney could take a bath.

Lousteau led Mahoney upstairs to a vacant apartment and showed him the bathtub.

"What happened to the people who used to live here?" Mahoney said, looking around at towels and bottles of perfume.

"They have fled the city, as have many people."

Lousteau left the apartment, and Mahoney put the plug in the tub and turned on the faucets. Cold water came out, but it wasn't icy and he thought he could handle it. He took off his filthy, smelly clothes and wished he had clean things to put on after the bath, but you can't have everything. When the tub was half-full of water, he stepped in. It took willpower and fortitude to lie down in the cold water, but once he was there his body adjusted to it and it didn't feel so bad.

He scrubbed himself down with soap and one of the washcloths hanging on the side of the tub, wondering who had lived in the apartment before it was vacated. The soap was perfumey and he figured it was a woman. He imagined what she looked like: tall and blonde with lips like strawberries. Then he thought of Shirley, although he knew he shouldn't. There was no future in that. He'd never see her again and he might as well get used to it.

He closed his eyes lazily and looked at his two knees rising out of the water like fleshy mountains. He imagined that the German fortress was on one of his knees, and the water around it was the bay of Cherbourg. The Germans had mined the harbor and were blowing up the docks, but underneath the pilings were torpedoes that would utterly destroy the harbor and keep the Allies from using it for months. Mahoney looked back and forth from the top of his knee to the dirty water in the bathtub, and suddenly a startling thought occurred to him.

He jumped out of the bathtub, wrapped himself in a towel, and jammed his wet feet into his shoes. Running out of the apartment, he descended the stairs until he reached the basement, and then burst into the room where Bulldog Boynton was sitting with Carpentier and Lousteau. They looked at him in alarm, as he dripped onto the floor. Carpentier's hand moved instinctively toward the pistol in his shoulder holster.

"I figured it out!" Mahoney said triumphantly.

"Figured what out?" Boynton asked.

"How to stop the Germans from detonating the torpedoes!" There was a bottle of wine on the table, and Mahoney moved it to the center. "Look!" he said, pointing to the cork in the bottle. "The fortress with the control room is up here, right?" He pointed to the table. “And the water of the bay is down here, right?” He looked at Boynton questioningly.

“I don’t follow you,” Boynton said.

“Think about it, Bulldog. There have to be wires connecting the detonation mechanisms in the control room with the torpedoes in the bay. This means that at one point the wires have to leave the fortress and travel the three blocks to the bay. So in other words, we don’t have to break into the fortress at all. We only have to find out where those wires are, and sabotage them.”

Boynton knitted together his eyebrows, then his face broke into a gruesome bulldog smile. “Good thinking, Mahoney! You may have solved the problem!”

Mahoney turned to Carpentier and told him the information in French.

“Very interesting,” Carpentier said, rubbing his chin with his fingers.

“Is there any way that we can find out the location of those wires?”

Carpentier thought for a few moments. “There is a possibility,” he said.

SIXTEEN

Lieutenant-General Carl Wilhem von Schlieben sat behind the desk in his office deep inside the Cherbourg fortress, and sipped a snifter of fine French cognac while calmly contemplating his prospects for survival. He was a haughty and aristocratic man, accustomed to playing polo and riding to hounds, and never dreamed that his career would come to its present sorry pass. Even through the thick walls of the fortress he could hear the American bombardment. His troops were moving back to Cherbourg now to make their last stand. Field Marshal Keitel had called him a few days ago and relayed the message from Adolf Hitler that von Schlieben should hold Cherbourg the way Field Marshal August Graf Neithardt von Gneisenau defended Kolberg during the Napoleonic Wars.

Von Schlieben sipped the brandy, feeling morose. He did not want to die and did not see the point of putting his life on the line for Cherbourg, a French city. If Cherbourg were in Germany it would be quite another matter, but it wasn't in Germany, so to hell with it.

On his desk was his last message from Field Marshal Rommel. It ordered him to defend Cherbourg "to the last bullet." Von Schlieben thought that was more like it. Better to the last bullet than to the last man. He'd fight until he was out of ammunition, and then put up the white flag. Of course he'd drag out the situation as long as he could, because he wouldn't want the SS to throw his wife and children into a concentration camp. He'd have to put up a good show to satisfy Hitler. It might be necessary to lie a little.

He raised the snifter of cognac to his nostrils, smelling its full-bodied aroma. As he was bringing the snifter to his lips, there was a terrific explosion somewhere in the fortress, and it shook as though an earthquake were taking place. Von Schlieben was startled, and spilled some of the cognac onto his tunic. He set the snifter on his desk and took out his white handkerchief, proceeding to wipe the stain away. While he was doing that, several more explosions rocked the fortress.

There was an urgent knock on his door.

Von Schlieben looked up. "Come in."

Lieutenant Weber, who was one of von Schlieben's staff aides, burst into the office and saluted wildly. "Herr Field Marshal, we have come under direct bombardment from enemy guns!" he reported.

"I know that," von Schlieben replied. "I have ears."

Lieutenant Weber stood trembling before von Schlieben, dots of perspiration on his face, not knowing what else to say.

"Don't be afraid, Lieutenant Weber," von

Schlieben said gently. "We'll be safe here."

"I was not worried about my safety!" Weber replied bravely, in a quavering voice.

"Of course not. Return to your post. Be sure to report any other drastic changes in circumstances."

"Yes, sir."

Lieutenant Weber saluted and left the office. Von Schlieben sipped some cognac as the fortress continued to shake with explosions. The situation is becoming serious, Schlieben thought. I wonder if they'll ask me to surrender? If they do, I'll turn them down, of course. And then I'll notify my engineers to blow up the harbor. If the Americans don't ask me to surrender, I'll blow it as soon as they near this fortress. Then I'll surrender.

Von Schlieben sipped his cognac and told himself to relax while he was still able, because he'd probably be in an American POW camp soon, and there'd certainly be no good cognac there. He hoped that the Americans would treat a Lieutenant General in the German Army with the proper respect, but doubted whether they would. America was a nation of mongrels, and you couldn't expect very much from people like that.

SEVENTEEN

A mile from the fortress, Lieutenant Helmut Keller of the *Wehrmacht* Engineers was having sexual intercourse with Francine Langlois in the bedroom of her little apartment on the Rue Crecy. They could hear artillery shells exploding in the distance, and that heightened their sexual pleasure. Curiously, although Francine was a spy for the *maquis*, she had come to love Keller. He was such a decent fellow, so affectionate, and so good-looking. She hoped that after the war was over they could get married, and was enough of a romantic to believe everything would work out all right in the end.

He started gulping and snorting as he always did when he was approaching orgasm, and she cupped her little hands on his ass to hold him close to her. She spread her legs wider, pointing her knees at the ceiling and shaking her fanny from side to side. Keller said a few garbled words of endearment to her throat and kissed her, as his balls exploded. He clicked his teeth and jerked his hips spasmodically, completely out of control, and his excitement set off her depth charges. The bed squeaked as they bounced around on top of it, clawing at each other like wild animals, drooling, slobbering, and grunting. If they could have seen themselves they would have been horrified.

All good things come to an end eventually, and so did their little bout of love. They lay exhausted in each other's arms for a while, as the window let in cool breezes, and they thought of how fortunate they were to be with each other.

After a while Helmut reached to the night table and got two cigarettes, lighting both of them in his mouth, and handing one to Francine. They smoked side by side on the pillow, and Francine wondered what strategy she should employ to secure from him the information she needed this time. Barrages of explosions shook the city, their sounds reverberating off the walls of the little bedroom.

Francine cuddled closer to him. "Are you sure we're safe here?" she asked, trembling a little.

"I told you it's quite safe here," he replied, blowing a column of cigarette smoke into the air. "Don't be afraid."

"But how can you be sure, Helmut?"

"Because this neighborhood has no strategic significance whatsoever. That's why I selected it for your apartment. Don't forget that I'm an engineer and I know how to read maps. The Americans would not waste shells bombing around here when they have more promising targets, such as Army barracks, military fortifications, artillery emplacements, and so forth, elsewhere."

"But what if a stray shell landed here?"

"Highly unlikely. Almost mathematically impossible. A stray shell *could* land here of course," he said pedantically, "but one also could land anywhere. Believe me my dear, this apartment is as safe as any apartment in Europe right now, and probably a lot safer than most of them."

She kissed his cheek, touching her small breast to his arm. "You're so intelligent, darling."

He accepted the kiss with aplomb. "I am fortunate to have a good education."

She returned to her position and puffed the cigarette. She could see the window from where she lay, and bright flashes of red light streaked across the night sky.

"I'm curious about something, Helmut," she said.

He laughed. "You want to ask about my other girlfriends again?"

"No, I believe that you don't have any other girlfriends."

"It's about time that you have come to trust me."

"Do you remember a few weeks ago," she said, "when you told me about the torpedoes you were using to blow up the harbor."

"Oh, you remembered that?"

"Yes, of course."

"Strange, I'd thought you'd forgotten, because you've never mentioned it since."

"Actually I haven't thought of it very much, but it isn't the sort of thing one forgets."

"No, I don't suppose it is."

"Well," she said, making swirls of smoke with the cigarette, "I've thought of something that I wonder if you've taken into consideration."

He chortled. "I assure you that I've taken

everything into consideration. Don't I always?"

"Well," she said, "have you thought of this? Your switch in the fortress is connected to the torpedoes in the harbor by wires, so what will happen if one of those American shells happens to land on the ground where the wires are run. That'll break the wires, won't it?"

He puffed his cigarette nonchalantly. "Of course it would break the wires, so naturally I've thought of it. The wires would have to be buried deep in the ground so that not only American shells wouldn't reach them, but also so that the *maquis* wouldn't be able to get to them."

"Oh, so you've dug a long trench from the fortress to the bay, and buried the wires?"

"No, no, no," he replied. "We wouldn't dare do that, because Cherbourg is full of *maquis* spies and they'd see what we were doing. Therefore we decided to run the wires through the sewer that goes from the fortress into the bay. The sewer is quite deep, so it is safe from enemy bombardment, and the local spies had no idea of what we were doing. We handled it rather well, don't you think?"

"That *is* clever," she said, cuddling him again.

"Yes, and this apartment is quite far from the waterfront, so when we throw the switch, you won't feel the explosion much here."

"And you, Helmut? Where will you be?"

"Deep in the fortress, and quite safe."

She hugged him and kissed his cheek. "I'm so worried about you."

"Oh, I'll be all right," he said.

"Please be careful, Helmut," she begged.

"I'll do everything I can. Now stop worrying. Worrying won't help."

He bent over her and kissed her nipple tenderly, and she wondered if there was anything she could do to safeguard Helmut's life, for she really was in love with him, and wanted him to be alive and in one piece when the war was over. As Helmut licked her nipple, an idea occurred to her. It was so obvious she was surprised she hadn't thought of it before.

EIGHTEEN

In the morning, American troops broke through German defenses, and entered the city of Cherbourg. Fierce house-to-house fighting ensued, as the citizens of the city who'd remained behind cowered in their cellars and prayed for divine intervention to save their lives.

American artillery battalions zeroed in on the fortress and subjected it to such an intense bombardment that poisonous fumes seeped into its uppermost corridors and rooms. Deep within the fortress, where the fumes had not yet gone, Lieutenant Colonel von Schlieben sat at his desk and drank a cup of coffee, while reading latest communiques from the front.

The situation looked bad, but was not perilous yet. He felt that he could put up a better fight if he had first-class German troops in his command, but his divisions were a hodge-podge of other units, and a majority of his troops were in their late thirties and early forties, less energetic and more cautious than their youthful American counterparts. Moreover, many of his soldiers weren't even Germans. They were Ukrainian Russians who hated Stalin and Communism and joined the German Army, winding up in France where they managed to commit numerous terrible atrocities against the French people.

How can anyone expect Russians in German uniforms to fight well against Americans in France? von Schlieben wondered. The war was getting crazy. Thank goodness it would be over for him soon.

There was a knock on the door.

"Come in."

Lieutenant Weber marched into the office, a document in his hand. He saluted von Schlieben, who saluted back casually.

"What is it this time?" von Schlieben asked.

Weber handed him the document. "The Americans are offering you the opportunity to surrender, sir."

Von Schlieben looked at the document. It was on the stationery of the United States VII Corps and was signed by Lieutenant General Joseph Lawton Collins. It said that von Schlieben and his troops had fought valiantly, but that the time had come for them to surrender. The document listed the surrender terms, which were quite generous actually, but von Schlieben felt that if he surrendered now, it wouldn't be so wonderful for his family in Germany, and moreover, the SS men prowling the fortress might shoot him as a traitor.

Von Schlieben looked up at Weber. "We're going to ignore this, Lieutenant. Send back no response whatsoever."

"But, sir," Weber said nervously, "the American commander quite rightly points out that we are in a hopeless situation, and further resistance is futile."

"I know how to read, Lieutenant Weber. You are

dismissed. Please send Major Obeldorf in to see me right away."

"Yes, sir."

Lieutenant Weber saluted, did an about-face, and marched out of the office. Von Schlieben looked at the surrender demand from General Collins again, shrugged fatalistically, and put it on a pile of other papers on his desk. Major Obeldorf, his chief engineering officer, entered his office and saluted.

"Have a seat, Major," von Schlieben said.

Major Obeldorf sat in one of the chairs in front of von Schlieben's desk. His head was shaved, he had a black mustache, and wore eyeglasses.

Von Schlieben leaned forward and folded his hands on his desk. "The crucial hour is rapidly approaching," he said. "I trust that all is in readiness?"

"You refer I assume to the demolitions?"

"Correct."

"All is in readiness."

"Are you sure that the bombing hasn't damaged any of your controls or the wires that lead to the torpedoes?"

"Quite sure. As you know, we have established an alarm system to inform us instantly if anything is wrong, and as you also know, the alarm system is manned twenty-four hours a day. If even one of those wires is severed in any way, a lightbulb will be activated on our control board. Since none of the lightbulbs have been activated, we must assume that the demolitions system still is intact."

Von Schlieben scratched his nose. "What if a light goes on?"

"We have a troop of combat engineers ready to enter the sewer system and effect repairs at a moment's notice."

"Good. If anything whatever happens to the demolitions system, I want to be notified immediately."

"Of course, sir."

"I want you and your section to be prepared to throw the switch at any time now, because as you know, the Americans are drawing closer."

"I know."

"That is all. Please return to your post."

"Yes, sir."

Obeldorf stood, saluted, and walked briskly out of the office. Von Schlieben raised his coffee cup to his lips and drank. The end was in sight, but he was ready for it. The next forty-eight hours should decide the issue. The tone of General Collins' letter was quite reasonable and decent. Von Schlieben felt confident that he'd be treated with all due courtesy when he became a prisoner of the Americans. You had to look at the bright side of things. The situation could be much worse.

NINETEEN

Francine entered the little basement room underneath the Fleur-de-Lis Cafe on the Rue Garonne. Carpentier sat around the big table with some of the *maquis* and the Americans who'd recently arrived. The room was filled with cigarette and cigar smoke, and she wondered how men could sit in such an atmosphere.

"You have the information?" Carpentier asked.

Francine took off her beret and ran her fingers through her blonde hair. "Yes."

Carpentier appeared impatient. "Please sit down and give it to us."

Francine sat next to the handsome young American whose hair was the same color as hers. "I'm not going to tell you unless you do a favor for me."

Carpentier blinked as though he didn't believe his ears. "What in the world are you talking about, woman!"

"You heard me very clearly I'm sure," she replied. "I'm not giving you any information whatever unless you do something for me first."

"What?"

She looked at her hands. "I want you to capture Helmut and bring him down here so that he'll be safe, because I'm afraid he'll be killed in all the fighting and bombing."

Carpentier looked at Mahoney in disbelief. Mahoney puffed his cigar and didn't change his expression because he wasn't surprised by what she'd said. He'd seen a lot of strange things happen in the war already and nothing surprised him anymore.

Carpentier turned to Francine. "Are you aware that you're risking the lives of innumerable French people, not to mention American and British soldiers, for the sake of this Kraut?"

She knitted together her eyebrows. "Don't call him that. He's a fine man."

"He's a Kraut!" Carpentier shouted, slamming his fist on the table.

"No he's not," Francine insisted. "He's a very fine man."

Mahoney leaned toward her. "I suppose you're in love with him?"

She looked at her hands and said softly: "Yes."

Mahoney turned to Carpentier. "It will be impossible to reason with her."

"What's going on?" asked Boynton, who didn't understand much French.

"She's in love with some fucking Kraut and she won't give us the information unless we kidnap him and bring him down here so that he'll be safe."

"Good grief," said Boynton.

"I never met a woman in my life who wasn't crazy."

"Can't they make her talk?"

"How can you make a woman talk if she doesn't want to talk? And how can you make one shut up if she doesn't want to shut up?"

Boynton ran his hand down his face. "I don't think I'm cut out for this behind-the-lines stuff."

Carpentier leaned toward Francine. "I don't suppose there's anything I can say or do to change your mind?"

"No."

Carpentier sighed. "Where can we find this filthy Kraut?" he asked.

TWENTY

It was three o'clock in the afternoon, and artillery shells were raining on the fortress. A lone figure in officer's uniform and helmet ran across the bomb-pitted courtyard to the front gate, where two guards huddled in a bunker covered with sandbags.

"It's him again," said one of the guards.

"I wonder where the hell he goes?" asked the other one.

"How should I know? Listen, it's your turn to go out and open the gate."

"Didn't I go last time?"

"No, I went last time."

"That's right, too."

The guard opened the door of the bunker and moved cautiously toward the gate, where Lieutenant Helmut Keller was standing, looking fearfully at the sky.

"Your pass, sir?"

Helmut showed it to him, and the guard opened the gate. Helmut ran across the street and hugged the buildings on the other side as he moved toward the part of town where Francine lived. The sidewalks were deserted and many of the nearby buildings had taken direct hits. It was possible that a shell would make a direct hit on him, but he had to see Francine. He was a young man in the prime of life and his blood was burning with love, therefore his judgment wasn't working at peak efficiency.

He moved quickly away from the fortress, because that's where the heaviest bombardment was taking place. Presumably the troops at the front were being bombarded too, but the front still was on the outskirts of the city. Francine's apartment wasn't in the line of the American advance, but it was possible that if he spent the night with her, the Americans might cut off his path of return in the morning. But he didn't care. The battle was nearing its end and the world was falling apart. The past several hours had been catastrophic, and he was ready to die if need be. He just wanted to spend a few more hours with his fair Francine.

He was now several blocks from the fortress, and stopped running. Looking around, seeing nothing threatening, he continued on his way to Francine's apartment. He thought of her blonde hair, long legs, and pert breasts. His penis became erect as he hurried through the streets of Cherbourg.

He made his way down the Rue Diane and across the Boulevard Saint Martin. In his knapsack he had two pounds of *bratwurst* and a large can of beans. That would be their dinner, and then they'd make love. How glorious that would be. If only they could be married and live in a city where there was no war. They would have children and be a proper family. The war was making life so difficult, but he realized that if it weren't for the war he never would have met the dear girl in the first place.

He turned onto her street and crossed over to the side where her building was. No one else was about and he felt as though he was the last man on earth. A few cars were parked on the street, and halfway down the block was an old black bread truck. He walked along quickly, anxious to see his darling, and when he came abreast of the old bread truck, he didn't notice the back door opening. Four men jumped out, and grabbed him before he knew what had happened. He opened his mouth to scream, but a big hand covered his lips and no sound would come out. The hand was so big it jammed against his nostrils, and he was afraid he'd suffocate. Terrified, struggling to get loose, he was carried by the four men to the back of the truck and pinned to the floor. They stuffed a gag into his mouth and tied his hands and feet as a fifth man sitting behind the wheel of the truck started it up and drove away.

TWENTY-ONE

The jeep came to a stop on a hill, and Lieutenant General Lightning Joe Collins got out, looking at Cherbourg through his binoculars. Other jeeps and trucks came to a stop behind it, and various officers and enlisted men unloaded. The convoy was the VII Corps tactical headquarters and Lightning Joe had moved it forward so that he could be closer to the front lines.

Through his binoculars he could see that part of the city was in flames and nearly all of it was obscured by smoke. His forces were steadily pushing the Germans back, and he was wondering whether to order a special attack to break through the German lines and storm the fortress. He raised his binoculars but the smoke was too thick to permit observance of the harbor, and the harbor was the key to the situation.

He returned his binoculars to their case and folded his arms, looking down at Cherbourg in its death throes. He could order the attack and it could easily take the fortress, but as soon as his troops got close he knew that von Schlieben would blow up the harbor. The main thing was to save the harbor if possible.

He'd received word that only five of the Rangers had made it through the German lines, and that they hadn't been able to sabotage the demolition system yet. He didn't know whether to wait for the Rangers to complete their mission, or take the city and accept the consequences. He was losing troops by hanging back and waiting, but more troops would be lost in the long run if the Germans destroyed the harbor.

Lightning Joe had to accept the fact that the Rangers might not be able to accomplish their mission. More than half of them hadn't even made it to Cherbourg. Maybe it was expecting too much of ordinary GIs to stop the Germans from blowing up the harbor. Maybe he should just order his troops ahead and take the damn port. There was no sense laying back forever like this taking casualties. The sooner he captured the port the sooner work could be begun on rebuilding the harbor.

He looked at his watch. His staff officers stood around, wondering what was going on in his mind. Lightning Joe counted hours and realized that the Rangers had been in Cherbourg for less than twenty-four hours, and maybe he was expecting too much from them. Maybe he should give them another twenty-four hours, and if they didn't carry out their mission by then, he'd pull out the stops and capture Cherbourg.

He turned to his legal officer, Major Mike Delsey. "Mike," he said, "do you think you can get a radio message in to the *maquis* in Cherbourg?"

"I think I can, sir," Delsey said.

"Tell them to notify our people there that if they don't knock out the demolitions system by 1200 hours tomorrow, we're going to move in and take the town."

"Yes, sir."

Major Delsey walked back to the truck that contained the headquarters radio system, and Lightning Joe called over his operations officer, Brigadier General Frank Knowland. "Frank," he said, "notify the corps commanders to pass on the word that I don't want the attack to be pressed too hard for the rest of today, but that they must prepare for a major assault tomorrow."

"Yes, sir," said General Knowland.

TWENTY-TWO

Mahoney and Cranepool carried Lieutenant Helmut Keller into the basement room underneath the Fleur-de-Lis Cafe. Helmut was as pale as a sheet, and he was nearly choking on the gag they'd stuffed into his mouth. He was certain that the *maquis* had captured him so that they could torture him to death. So frightened was he that it took a few seconds before he recognized Francine sitting at the table with a bunch of grubby Frenchmen who looked like *maquis*. "What are you doing here?" he demanded of her, but the gag was in his mouth and no sound came out.

"Darling!" she said with a big smile, getting up and rushing toward him, embracing him and kissing his cheek.

Carpentier made a face. "I've never seen anything so disgusting in my life!"

"Stick around," Mahoney replied cynically.

She pulled the gag out of Helmut's mouth. "Are you all right?" she asked.

"What's going on!" he screamed.

"Don't worry," she said, "you're safe."

Helmut looked down at the faces of the *maquis*

members and the Americans whom he thought were in the *maquis*. He didn't feel safe at all. "What are they going to do with me?"

"Nothing."

What are you doing here with them?"

She smiled sadly. "My dear," she said, "I happen to be a spy for the *maquis*."

"WHAT!"

"Calm down."

"A spy for the *maquis*?" he asked in a daze.

"Yes, my dear Helmut."

His eyes filled with tears. "You've never loved me," he said weakly. "You were only using me to get information. I can see it all now. I've been a dupe."

She embraced him as he stood with his hands and feet tied. "It's true that at first I was trying to wheedle information out of you, but then I fell in love with you, Helmut. I've had them bring you here so that you'll be safe."

Mahoney looked at Carpentier. "I can't take much more of this shit," he said.

"It's completely disgusting and obnoxious," Carpentier agreed. "To think that a fine French girl is in love with a German when Germans are killing Frenchmen every day and putting them into concentration camps."

Francine looked at Carpentier, her eyes ablaze. "Helmut never put anybody in a concentration camp! They drafted him into the Army and what was he supposed to do, say no?"

"I think I'm going to throw up," Mahoney said.

"What are they saying?" Boynton asked.

"A lot of bullshit," Mahoney replied in English.

"We don't have time for bullshit, Mahoney. We've got to find out where those wires are."

"That's right, too." Mahoney looked at Carpentier. "Can we find out where the wires are?"

"Ah, yes," Carpentier replied. "I almost forgot." He looked at Francine. "We have kept our side of the bargain by bringing your worthless Kraut boyfriend here. Now it's your turn to fulfill your side of the bargain. Where have they buried the wires that will detonate the torpedoes in the harbor?"

She placed her hands on her hips and glowered at him. "You all think you're so smart and yet you haven't figured it out although it's as obvious as the nose on your face. They've run the wires through the sewer that goes from the fortress to the bay, you fool!"

Carpentier's jaw dropped open.

"Very interesting," Mahoney said. "Does anybody know where that sewer is?"

Cranepool pointed at Helmut. "I'll bet he does."

"I refuse to answer any questions," Helmut said. "I'm a prisoner of war and all I have to tell you are my name, rank, and serial number."

Lousteau laughed darkly. "You'll sing a different tune after we put your balls in a vise."

Francine barred her teeth like a wild tigress. "You'll do no such thing!" she screamed.

"We'll put your damn head in a vise with his balls if you don't lower your voice!" Lousteau replied.

Francine dived on him, but Mahoney stood up and caught her in mid-air. "I think we should put her and her Kraut in another room someplace, so we can make a few basic strategic plans," he said as she struggled to break out of his grip.

"You're right," Carpentier said. He ordered two of his men to take Francine and Helmut down the hall to another room and maintain a close guard on them. The two men picked up Helmut and carried him out of the room, as Francine followed.

"Don't hold him too tightly," she said. "Don't hurt him."

They left the room and Boynton looked at Mahoney. "Would you mind telling me what the fuck is going on here?"

"The wires are in a sewer. Now all we have to do is find out where the sewer is." Mahoney turned to the others. "Does anyone here have any idea where that sewer is?"

The Frenchmen looked at each other and shrugged.

"Is there any way we can find out?" Mahoney asked.

One of the Frenchmen leaned forward and folded his hands on the table. "I used to work in the City Hall, and I know that blueprints of the sewer system are stored in one of the record rooms. If the City Hall still is there, the blueprints should be too."

Mahoney looked at Carpentier. "I think some of us had better go over there right away and get those blueprints."

"I agree," Carpentier replied. He stood and called the names of four of his men, who also got to their feet. They left the room, and Boynton turned to Mahoney.

"Now what's going on?" he asked.

"They're going to get the blueprints of the sewer system."

"Oh, I see," Boynton said. "Boy, I wish I knew French so that I could understand what was going on."

"I wish you knew French too," Mahoney said, because he was getting tired of doing the translations.

Mahoney puffed the cigar that he'd bummed off one of the Frenchmen, and hoped that the blueprints of the sewer system would be intact, but on the other hand, he didn't look forward to crawling through the shit and garbage of the sewer system that evening. He looked into Boynton's eyes.

"I hate this fucking war," he said.

"Mahoney," Boynton replied, "if there were no more wars and no more armies, guys like you would starve to death."

"Fuck you, sir," Mahoney said, puffing his cigar.

TWENTY-THREE

It was seven o'clock in the evening, and the fortress was wreathed with smoke. American artillery shells continued dropping on the fortress, and its ramparts had become rubble. Wounded German soldiers were being moved to the lower chambers because the upper ones were filled with poisonous fumes. General von Schlieben paced back and forth in front of his desk and realized that the time had come to blow up the harbor and then raise the white flag of surrender. He'd fought the good fight and his soldiers had nothing to be ashamed of. They all could get a peaceful night of rest as POWs, and in the morning perhaps he could breakfast with General Collins, and discuss the great battles of history.

But first he had to blow up the harbor. He buttoned his tunic up to his neck and smoothed the front. His black boots were highly polished. Placing his hat on his head, he lifted his riding crop off his desk, smacked it against his leg, and marched out of his office.

The next room was the conference room, where he

held a conference with his staff every day at nine o'clock in the morning, and over the past week the conferences had become progressively gloomier, with dispiriting news coming in from all fronts, and impossible orders being received over the radio from Berlin. Well, von Schlieben thought, that's just about all over. I'll throw the switch myself, and after everything settles down, I'll send an emissary to General Collins. His surrender requests were worded most decently. I'm sure he's a gentleman such as myself.

General von Schlieben opened the door to the large office that had been converted into the control room for the special demolition program. He confidently strode into the room, heading for the main switch, and nearly had a heart attack when he saw that the room was filled with SS men in full battle gear.

"Going someplace?" asked Colonel Feldheim, commander of the local SS Gestapo detachment, as he arose from a chair.

Von Schlieben swallowed hard. Although he outranked Feldheim, the SS colonel had the authority to ship him to a concentration camp or have him shot on the spot. "I just thought I'd check the controls," von Schlieben said, "because the time is drawing near for me to blow up the harbor."

Feldheim was slim, with a black mustache similar to Adolf Hitler's. He had a large nose and von Schlieben always thought he looked a little Jewish. "You needn't concern yourself about the harbor any more," he said in his oily voice. "My headquarters has just received a radio communications from

Berlin. The Fuehrer has ordered me to take charge of the harbor demolitions."

"I see," said von Schlieben. "You have a copy of the orders for me?"

"Certainly."

Feldheim took out the orders and showed them to von Schlieben. They appeared to be in order. Von Schlieben handed them back to Feldheim. "I trust that a copy will be sent to me for my files."

"One is on the way, if it hasn't been delivered to one of your staff officers already."

"I'll check," von Schlieben said icily.

"I think you should. Your headquarters always has been bedeviled by sloppy staff work."

"I beg your pardon!" von Schlieben declared.

"It's the truth," Feldheim said with a yawn. "Everybody knows it. Even the Fuehrer does."

"The Fuehrer?"

"Of course. Everybody knows that he wanted someone stronger in command here."

"I'm surprised he didn't appoint you," von Schlieben said drily.

"He could have done worse," Feldheim said.

Feldheim's SS men giggled and chortled at that one, causing von Schlieben's temperature to rise.

"I'm not so sure that he could have done worse," von Schlieben snapped, smacking his riding crop against his leg. "May I inquire when you intend to blow up the harbor?"

"When this room is in danger of being destroyed or captured by the Americans."

"Well," von Schlieben said, "since the responsibility has been taken out of my hands, I won't concern myself with it anymore. I wish you a good day, Colonel Feldheim."

"The best of days to you, General von Schlieben," Feldheim said with a wry smile.

Von Schlieben turned and swaggered out of the control room, slapping his riding crop against his leg. He strutted across the conference room, entered his office, and collapsed at his desk. Opening the bottom drawer, he took out his bottle of cognac, which now was only one-quarter full. He unscrewed the cork and raised the bottle to his mouth, tossing back his head and taking a healthy swig. The fortress trembled with explosions, and von Schlieben could hear their muffled sounds. He returned the bottle to his desk drawer and closed it, wondering seriously for the first time whether or not he'd survive the war.

TWENTY-FOUR

It was eight o'clock in the evening. In the deserted streets of northwest Cherbourg, an old black bread truck turned a corner onto the Rue Vendome and rolled slowly down the block. It was dark and no streetlights were on, the local power station having been reduced to rubble by American bombardments.

The bread truck rolled over a manhole cover halfway down the block and came to a stop just beyond it. The rear door of the bread truck opened and Mahoney stepped out, a crowbar in his hand. Behind him were Bulldog Boynton, Cranepool, Carpentier, Private Gomez, Sergeant Newell, Soulanges, and two other Frenchmen named Langeais and Chaperon. They all carried captured German submachine guns or had them strapped to their backs.

Mahoney jammed the crowbar into the edge of the manhole cover and pried it up. Cranepool and Chaperon grabbed the manhole and pulled it away. The odor of shit and muck came up to them from the sewer. They fastened bandanas in front of their noses and mouths to keep out some of the stink, and

Mahoney was the first one to climb down the steel rungs into the sewer. The bottom was ten feet down, and ankle deep with oozy gunk. The others followed him down the ladder and joined him in the sewer, while on the street, a Frenchman replaced the manhole cover, got into the bread truck, and drove away.

All the men in the sewer carried knapsacks filled with explosives. Canteens of water were hooked to their belts. They took out their flashlights and flashed them around, looking gloomily at the concrete pipe, ten feet in diameter that they were inside.

Carpentier shone his flashlight on the map of the Cherbourg sewer system that they'd taken from City Hall. "This way," he said.

They followed him through the mire and abominations that filled the sewer. Their footsteps echoed throughout the tunnels and passageways of the sewer system, making it appear as though patrols of men were marching about all around them.

They came to an intersection of sewer pipes, and Carpentier led them to the left. They were about a mile from the section of the sewer where the wires were located, and hoped to arrive there within an hour. There was no way of knowing whether or not that section of the sewer was guarded, but they'd worry about that when they got there. A more frightening possibility was that the Germans might blow up the harbor while they were down in the sewer. The explosion could rupture the sewer system, causing water from the bay to pour in and drown them like rats.

There's no point in thinking about depressing

things like that, Mahoney figured as he trudged with the others through the sewer. The powerful stench was seeping through the red bandana over his nose and mouth, making him nauseous. Rats skittered around the walls of the sewer and he thought that this would be a helluva place to die, in a river of shit with rats nibbling on your fingers.

He decided that this particular mission was the worst thing that had happened to him since he joined the Army. It wasn't so bad fighting like an ordinary soldier in a normal battle, but this sewer business was horrible and nightmarish. He told himself that if he got out of this mission alive, he'd transfer to a regular infantry outfit. Weird assignments no longer seemed interesting and glamorous to him, and he realized that they increased his chances of getting knocked off. He'd be much better off in a regular infantry line company. So what if the soldiers weren't as good as rangers? He knew how to watch his ass and that's what he intended to do for the rest of the war, if only he survived this sewer.

A few steps behind him, young Cranepool slogged through the gunk at the bottom of the sewer. He carried his submachine gun with its buttplate snug against his hip and its barrel pointed up at the ceiling. The sewer didn't bother him as much as Mahoney because he'd been shoveling shit on the farm for most of his life and was used to it. He was thinking that when this mission was over he'd talk to Bulldog Boynton about becoming a buck sergeant. He'd have enough time in grade next month, and wanted very much to become a sergeant because everyone knew that sergeants were the backbone of the Army. As a sergeant, it would be easier for him to go get into OCS. They might even send him to West Point! Cranepool thought his future in the Army looked extremely bright. When he returned home in his officer's uniform someday, the local girls would cream in their pants.

Beside Carpentier at the head of the column, Bulldog Boynton trudged along stolidly, ever on the alert for strange sounds and unusual shadows, a professional soldier to the core. His mind was devoid of any thoughts not connected with the mission he was presently on. He figured the best way to fight an enemy in a sewer was to get down into the muck and take the battle to him. As your own men were killed, you'd use their bodies as barricades. You'd send detachments through the sewer system to encircle your foe. And you'd fight until you were killed, because a good soldier never surrendered.

The group of men made their way through the sewer system of Cherbourg, moving ever closer to the length of pipe that passed from the fortress to the bay. They heard the faint sounds of explosions far above them, and the pouring of water in the far reaches of the sewer system. Their searchlights flashed before them like an amorphous creature with a hundred eyes. Certain sections of the sewer smelled so terrible that they gagged and tried to hold their breaths. To keep from throwing up, Mahoney forced himself to think of flowers and babies, of the roller coaster at Coney Island and Glenn Miller's orchestra playing "*Pennsylvania Six-five-oh-oh-oh,*" and of the long supple legs of Shirley the nurse. He realized now for the first time that he'd never even found out her last name.

Carpentier held up his hand, and the column behind him stopped. He took out the map and studied it in the light of his flashlight. "We're almost there," he said. "Be on the lookout for Germans."

They moved out again, holding their submachine guns at the ready, listening and watching for signs of German guards. Mahoney hoped there were no guards and no alarm system, because a firefight in a sewer would be a horrible thing. But he doubted that there'd be any serious trouble. The Germans probably never dreamed that someone would find out their nasty little secret.

They came to another sewer intersection, and Carpentier led them to the right. "The fortress should be directly overhead," Carpentier said. "Keep your eyes peeled for trouble." They followed Carpentier in the new direction, the sounds of their movements echoing all around them. After fifty yards they came to another intersection, where a pipe angled into the one they were in. "That's the pipe from the fortress," Carpentier told them. "The wires for the demolitions should be coming right through here. Roll up your sleeves and look for it."

Mahoney frowned as he took off his watch and put it in his pocket. He rolled up his sleeves, bent over, and reached into the warm slime, feeling for the wires. His fingers touched chicken bones, orange peels and an old shoe swimming in the muck, but no wires.

"I've got something!" said Langeais.

He took a grip onto something and pulled it up. They shone their flashlights on it, and it was a rubber-sheathed cable about six inches thick.

"That must be it," Carpentier said. "Get the explosives ready."

They took off their packs and unloaded the sticks of TNT, laying them on and around the cable. Mahoney had a special blasting cap that would work underwater and give them thirty seconds to get away before it blew. He jammed it into the end of the topmost stick of TNT and looked up at Carpentier. "Ready?"

"Yes," said Carpentier. He looked at Boynton. "Ready?"

"Let's do it," Boynton replied.

"Okay," Mahoney said, "the rest of you might as well go back and get behind that last intersection we passed. When you're all there, give me three dots from a flashlight, and I'll trip the cap. Then I'll joint you."

Carpentier and Boynton nodded. The men picked up their empty knapsacks and splashed back to the intersection, while Mahoney watched them go, wondering why he'd volunteered to be the one who stayed behind. What an asshole I'm turning out to be, he thought, but he realized that he'd volunteered because the only way to make sure a job was done right was to do it himself. He watched the others recede down the sewer tunnel, their flashlights blazing a path before them. Taking his watch out of his pocket, he saw that it was a few minutes after nine o'clock. He hoped the cable beneath his feet indeed contained the wires that ran to the network of torpedoes in the harbor, and he hoped the TNT and blasting cap would work the way they were supposed to. He felt a little ill at ease, because the sewer job had gone too smoothly. It seemed as though the Germans should have had some guards or something in the sewer to make sure the cable remained secure, but maybe they had been overconfident, never dreaming that a ragged bunch of *maquis* and American troopers would be able to sabotage it.

The tunnel went dark ahead of him as Carpentier and the others rounded the corner. Then Mahoney saw three quick flashes from one of their flashlights. It was time to blow up the tunnel. He made sure his pack was adjusted tightly on his back, worked the muscles in his shoulders, then bent over and pulled the little string on the blasting cap. The cap made a *snap* sound, and now it was activated. It would blow in thirty seconds, and Mahoney started running to the bend ahead, stretching his long legs out underneath him, slicing the fetid air with the blades of his hands while counting off the seconds. His big feet splashed through the muck and sent it flying in all directions. A frightened rat squeaked loudly and fled back toward the TNT, and Mahoney kept on going, hoping he'd reach the bend before the count of thirty, because he didn't want to drop down onto his stomach in the muck of the sewer. His exertion caused him to breathe heavily, filling his lungs with the smelly air, and he felt like vomiting. At the count of twenty-three he made it to the bend and ducked behind it with the others.

They pressed their backs to the wall of the tunnel and he huddled in with them. The TNT would go off any second now, and he had the mad thought that it might weaken the entire sewer system and bring the fortress crashing down on their heads. Sweat dripped down his forehead to the bandana over his mouth and nose, and he told himself to calm down.

The TNT detonated with a violent ear-splitting sound, and the shock wave was like a slap against Mahoney's face. Hunks of metal and rock came flying past the tunnel they were sheltering themselves in, carrying clumps of shit and gunk with it. They pressed their backs against the wall of the sewer and heard debris falling everywhere. Clouds of smoke furled back toward them, and they remained still for a few moments, waiting for everything to settle down.

At a signal from Carpentier they came out from their hiding place and shined their flashlights in the direction of the explosion. They saw smoke and a huge pile of rubble that made the sewer impassable. Mahoney smiled with satisfaction. It was a tremendous mess and the Germans wouldn't be able to get through it for a couple of days and maybe longer because they were under attack and probably short on manpower. It would take them several days to repair the cable, but Lightning Joe Collins would have Cherbourg in his back pocket by then, and all the Germans would be POWs or dead.

Carpentier motioned with his hand, "Let's get out of here," he said.

TWENTY-FIVE

In the control room, Colonel Max Feldheim sat in a comfortable leather chair and read the latest issue of *Schwarz Corps,* the weekly newspaper of the SS. Around him sat the men of his detachment, talking softly, playing cards, and reading books obtained earlier in the day from the library.

At the control panel, Private Wilhelm Haufholz was jolted by the sight of all the emergency lights going on at once. Simultaneously, the faint sound of an explosion could he heard far beneath them.

"Sir!" shouted Private Haufholz. "All the lights are on!"

"All the lights are on?" Feldheim asked incredulously, standing and walking toward the control panel. He blinked his eyes and saw that all the lights were indeed on. He stood next to the control panel and wrinkled his brow. "Could there be a short circuit in the wires?" he asked Private Haufholz, who had been an electrician in civilian life.

"A short circuit couldn't do this, sir. A short circuit would blow a fuse." He pointed to the fuse panel. "As you can see, sir, none of the fuses are blown."

"Hmmm," said Colonel Feldheim. "I wonder what it is?"

"I thought I heard an explosion at the same time the lights went on, sir."

"An explosion? That shouldn't be considered unusual," Feldheim said. "Explosions are taking place around here all the time."

"But not underneath the fortress, sir."

"Underneath the fortress, you say?"

"Yes, sir."

An SS sergeant stepped forward. "I thought I heard an explosion from underneath the fortress too, sir."

"So did I," said a corporal.

Feldheim straightened up and set his jaw. Could saboteurs have blown up the cable? "Klopper!" he shouted to one of his sergeants. "Take five men down to the sewer and see if anything's happened down there!"

"Yes, sir."

"Hurry!"

"Yes, sir."

Sergeant Klopper selected five volunteers and ran out one of the doors with them. Feldheim paced back and forth hoping that the tunnel was intact, because if the *maquis* had sabotaged it, his career would take a nosedive and perhaps his life would come to a sudden horrible end. He clicked his teeth together and tried to figure out what to do.

He turned to another of his sergeants. "I'm going to see General von Schlieben," he said. "If Klopper returns before I come back, send him in to me in General von Schlieben's office."

"Yes, sir!"

Colonel Feldheim adjusted his hat and marched out of the control room. He headed toward von Schlieben's office and knocked on the door.

"Come in," said von Schlieben.

Feldheim charged into the office and saw von Schlieben sitting behind his desk writing something. "Heil Hitler!" Feldheim cried, throwing out his hand in the Hitler salute.

Von Schlieben looked up from his desk. "Heil Hitler," he said without much enthusiasm. "To what do I owe the pleasure of this visit?"

"General von Schlieben!" Feldheim announced. "All the lights on the control panel are on!"

Von Schlieben's jaw dropped open like the bottom of a steam shovel. "All of them, you say?"

"Yes, sir."

Von Schlieben thought about it for a few moments, and then smiled. "How very interesting," he said.

"Interesting!" Feldheim screamed. "You call it interesting! Is that all you can think of saying!"

"But my dear colonel," von Schlieben said suavely, "the control panel is no longer my responsibility, it's yours now, remember? Isn't that what you told me earlier today? All I can say is that you have my deepest sympathy if the cable should happen to have been cut by the *maquis*, because the Fuehrer won't be very happy about that, I assure you. It's too bad that you didn't throw the switch while you had the chance, but I'm afraid it's probably too late for that now, eh?"

"Too late?" Feldheim asked. The thought occurred to him that maybe some kind of strange electrical malfunction had taken place, but that the torpedoes still could be blown. Perhaps he should go back and throw the switch to make sure. He cursed himself for not throwing the switch earlier when he had the chance.

"Did you say something?" von Schlieben asked pleasantly.

"I'll speak with you about this matter later," Feldheim replied. "That is all for now, General von Schlieben. Heil Hitler!"

Feldheim dashed out of von Schlieben's office and returned to the control room, where the SS men were crowded around the panel, watching the lights.

"Get out of my way you fools!" Feldheim shouted, pushing them out of his way. He dived at the control panel, grabbed the four-inch black wood handle of the master switch and slammed it into the copper clips that made the complete electrical connection.

Nothing happened, and his heart sank. If the cable was working properly, he would have heard a huge explosion that would have rocked the fortress like an earthquake, but there was nothing, not even a little pop, not even the slightest tremor. Feldheim saw a vision of himself standing before a firing squad.

Sergeant Klopper burst into the control room and threw the Hitler salute. "My Colonel," he shouted. "There has been a major explosion in the sewer tunnel!"

Feldheim closed his eyes and the blood drained

from his face. The *maquis* had sabotaged the sewer tunnel. He wished this was a nightmare from which he'd soon awaken. "How extensive is the damage?" he asked, opening his eyes.

"It looks pretty bad, sir. The tunnel's completely blocked off. A great deal of explosive material must have been used."

Feldheim smashed his fist into the palm of his hand. He should have posted guards in the sewer, but he hadn't thought it necessary. He'd never dreamed that the *maquis* would find out about the demolition operation, and wondered exactly how they did find out.

"Perhaps we can catch them, sir," said Sergeant Klopper.

"Catch who?"

"The *maquis*. They still might be down in the sewer system."

"You think so?" Feldheim asked.

"It's possible, sir. Of course, they might have planted the explosives earlier in the day and left a time delay fuse, but I doubt if they'd take the chance of waiting that long. I think they'd blow it on the spot and then try to get away."

Feldheim clicked his teeth. "Yes, of course. You're completely right. They're probably down there right now and if we move fast we can catch them. Follow me!"

Feldheim drew his service revolver and dashed out of the room. The SS detachment followed him as he pushed chairs out of his way in the conference room and ran down the corridor outside. They hopped down three flights of stairs, sped down another hall, through a door, and ran into the courtyard just as an artillery shell made a direct hit on the front gate, filling the air with flying debris.

Feldheim and his detachment dropped behind the low stone wall that lined the courtyard, and when the smoke cleared, Feldheim jumped to his feet and yelled: "Follow me!"

They ran across the courtyard and jumped over the smoking chunks of concrete and twisted steel that once had been the gate. Charging into the cobblestoned street, Feldheim looked both ways, wondering where there was a manhole that would give them entrance to the sewer system. He paused in the middle of the street, wondering which way to go.

"What are you looking for, sir?" asked Sergeant Klopper.

"A manhole, you idiot!"

"That's what I thought, sir. There's one this way." The sergeant pointed to the right.

They ran to the right and fifty yards beyond the first intersection they came upon a manhole cover. Feldheim looked down at it excitedly, his lips flecked with spittle. "Open it up!" he screamed.

"I think we should be quiet, sir," said Sergeant Klopper, "so that maybe we can take them by surprise."

"Of course. Be quiet all of you. We must try to ambush them."

Sergeant Klopper drew his bayonet from his scabbard and told three of his men to do likewise. They got on their knees beside the manhole cover and stuck their bayonets around the edge, prying it up slowly. An artillery shell landed on the roof of a building across the street, and a split second later, another landed near the front gate of the fortress. The air was filled with smoke and the sky flickered with the light of explosions all around them. The sound of continual bombardment was almost deafening.

When the manhole cover was pried up a few inches, Klopper caught it with his fingers and uncovered the manhole carefully so that he wouldn't make much noise. Feldheim was the first one in the hole, descending the iron rungs with his service revolver still in his hand. Klopper was next, and then the others. The odor was horrible, and when Feldheim got to the bottom he pinched his nose with his fingers. The detachment descended the iron rungs and stood silently around Feldham, listening to sounds in the tunnel.

"I think I hear them." Feldheim whispered.

"Yes, that way," Klopper replied, pointing.

"I knew they couldn't be far away. Everybody be still."

They froze and listened to the sound of footsteps and splashing somewhere in the distance. Feldheim smiled. If he could kill them all, maybe he could redeem himself. Maybe he could blame the blow-up of the tunnel on von Schlieben and the engineers. Maybe his future wasn't so bleak after all.

"This way," he said, advancing gingerly toward the sound of the footsteps. "I think we might be able to trap them."

TWENTY-SIX

Not far away, Mahoney and the others were trudging through a sewer tunnel. They were on their way to a certain manhole cover near which the bread truck was supposed to be parked.

The stink of the tunnel was driving Mahoney nuts. He was hallucinating a movie of himself crawling up through a manhole cover into the sweet night air of Cherbourg. What a wonderful moment that would be. He had made the firm decision that as soon as he got back to the Twenty-Third Rangers, he'd put in for a transfer to an ordinary infantry regiment in an ordinary line division, and spend the rest of the war fighting above ground like a human being, instead of in these strange situations behind enemy lines. He thought he'd have a better chance of surviving the war that way, and he wouldn't have to go down into any more damned sewers.

He paused for a cigar, hoping that the smoke would cancel out some of the sewer's smell. Taking the cigar out of his shirt pocket, he peeled off the wrapper and lit it with his trusty old Zippo. He puffed the cigar greedily and was pleased to notice that it did cut the stink of the sewer a little. He wished he'd had the idea before. He might have saved himself some discomfort.

Puffing the cigar and taking long strides to catch up with the rest, he wondered how close they were to the manhole cover. He decided to catch up with Carpentier and ask him, when suddenly a barrage of light weapons fire opened up in front of them.

The SS men had submachine guns and rifles, and their opening burst cut down Carpentier and Bulldog Boynton, who'd been leading the men through the sewer. It also brought down two of the Frenchmen and Sergeant Newell, who had been close by.

At the first sound of the fire, Mahoney dropped to his stomach in the muck and shit. Looking over the other men who'd either been hit or were taking cover also, he saw flashes of light coming from both sides of the tunnel not more than twenty feet away. The Germans or whoever was there had positioned themselves on either side of an intersection and were firing from behind the walls of the tunnel.

Thinking and moving quickly, Mahoney took a hand grenade from his pocket, pulled the pin, and lobbed it into the center of the intersection. Then he held his breath and ducked his head into the filth of the sewer, because that was preferable to getting it blown off.

The hand grenade exploded, filling the air with smoke and shrapnel. Mahoney raised himself from the muck, took out another hand grenade, pulled the pin, and hurled it forward. It exploded like the first one, and Mahoney jumped up with his submachine gun. "CHARGE!" he screamed.

A few other bodies got up and followed him as he ran the final twenty feet to the intersection, spraying both sides of the tunnel with submachine gun fire. When he reached the intersection he put his back against the wall on one side of it and fired into the other side, while across from him, another member of his demolition party did the same thing, firing into the opening beside Mahoney.

Mahoney emptied a clip into the dark morass of the sewer, then ejected it and rammed a fresh clip in. "Hold your fire," he said to the person opposite him, and Cranepool stepped out of the dark shadows, his submachine gun smoking.

Mahoney stepped into the tunnel that entered the intersection from the left, and saw German meat and bones. Bending down, he noticed that they were wearing SS uniforms. It had been a clumsy ambush, doomed to failure, Mahoney thought. The SS had the element of surprise but they didn't have enough men and they weren't positioned right. They should have attacked from the front and the back but they hadn't and it was tough shit for them. Mahoney stomped around the legs and torsos no longer connected to each other, until he was satisfied they all were dead. There were about five of them but it was difficult to tell because the hand grenades had ripped them to shreds. Mahoney turned around and walked toward Cranepool.

"Anything over there?" Mahoney asked.

"Only dead Krauts," Cranepool answered.

"How many?"

"It's hard to say."

"About how many?"

"A few I guess."

"Let's go back."

They walked back to the others and saw Private Gomez, Soulanges and Langeais halfway between them and the ones who'd been hit. Mahoney swallowed hard because he realized now for the first time that Bulldog Boynton had been one of the casualties. Grinding his teeth together, he walked in long strides to the morass of bodies lying in the muck. He found Boynton and pulled him out of the shit, laying him against the dry curve of the sewer wall. Blood oozed from three holes in Boynton's chest, and a turd was in his hair. Mahoney pressed his ear to Boynton's chest, but could hear no heartbeat.

"You poor son of a bitch," Mahoney said, looking at the corpse of his former C.O. They'd been through a lot of war together, but now the war was over for Bulldog Boynton.

Mahoney wasn't much of a Catholic anymore, but he crossed himself anyway. Then he realized that they'd all better get moving, because more SS men might be on the way. "We'd better get out of here," he said. "Anybody know which way to go?"

The others shrugged and looked at each other with blank expressions on their faces.

"I think that way," said Soulanges, pointing in one direction.

"No, this way," said Langeais, pointing in a different direction.

"Assholes," Mahoney mumbled.

He sloshed through the muck and bent over Carpentier's body, picking it up and leaning it against the curved sewer wall. Reaching into Carpentier's jacket pocket, he took out the sewer system map that they'd got at City Hall. It was wet on the outside but only damp inside, as Mahoney unfolded it. Carpentier had made a big X with a pencil at the location of the manhole cover where the bread truck was waiting. Mahoney studied the map and oriented himself in the sewer system. He figured out which way they were supposed to go.

"Let's get out of here," he said.

He picked up Bulldog Boynton and threw him over his shoulder. Cranepool lifted Sergeant Newell, and Soulanges and Langeais carried the bodies of Carpentier and Newell. They began to move in the direction of the SS men who had tried to ambush them.

"HALT!"

The voice came from behind them, and Mahoney knew that when somebody told you to halt, that was the time to take cover. "GET DOWN!" he shouted, dropping Bulldog Boynton's body to the bottom of the sewer tunnel and getting behind it.

"SURRENDER — YOU DON'T HAVE A CHANCE!" screamed Colonel Feldheim, who had split his SS detachment into two squads, one to ambush the fleeing *maquis,* and the other to encircle them.

"FUCK YOU!" Mahoney hollered, ramming a bullet into the chamber of his submachine gun and opening fire.

A noisy firefight broke out in the sewer. Mahoney and his men poured submachine-gun fire at the SS, who huddled behind the walls of another sewer intersection, and returned the fire, their bullets ripping into the dead bodies in front of Mahoney, Cranepool, and the others.

Mahoney had no more hand grenades, and neither did anyone else. He realized that the longer they stayed there, the more likely that German reinforcements would arrive. He gritted his teeth and fired his submachine gun over the body of Bulldog Boynton as he tried to think of a plan. Langeais screamed and fell back, a bullet tearing off the top of his head. Mahoney realized he only had one hope and he'd better get it rolling right away.

"Cranepool," he said, still firing his submachine gun at the Germans.

"Yeah, Sarge?"

"Take the map out of my pocket and lead the others to the truck. I'll cover you."

"But what about you, Sarge?" Cranepool asked, also firing nonstop at the Germans.

"Don't worry about me. Get the map and get the fuck out of here. Go back to the cafe and call headquarters on the radio. Tell them that the German demolition system has been knocked out. Got all that?"

"But Sarge . . ."

"I asked if you got that, Corporal!"

"Got it, Sarge."

"Then get your fucking ass in gear."

"Hup, Sarge."

Cranepool took the map from inside Mahoney's shirt while Mahoney continued to spray the tunnel with bullets. The others had heard what Mahoney said and huddled around Cranepool.

"Good luck, Sarge," Cranepool said, touching his

hand to Mahoney's shoulder.

"I said get fucking going!"

"Hup, Sarge."

Mahoney lay behind Boynton's mangled shoulder and fired his bucking, howling submachine gun as Cranepool led Gomez and Soulanges back to the intersection where the dead Germans were. Bullets whizzed around the sewer tunnel, ricocheting off the walls. When Cranepool was only a few feet from the intersection, one of the ricocheting bullets hit Gomez in the back, and the young Mexican-American stumbled and pitched forward onto his face. Cranepool and Soulanges ducked behind the intersection wall, and they were safe. Cranepool paused for a moment, not wanting to leave Mahoney alone, but orders were orders and he had to carry them out.

"This way," he said to Soulanges, moving in the direction of the manhole where the truck was waiting. From behind, he could hear the rattle of submachine-gun bullets in the tunnel where Mahoney was holding off the Germans single-handedly.

TWENTY-SEVEN

Mahoney ejected an empty clip and slammed a new one into his submachine gun. He lifted it over Boynton's bullet-riddled corpse and fired a burst toward the Germans, then reached out with his big right hand and lifted the body of Langeais, putting it on top of Boynton and providing a little more protection.

He raised his submachine gun again and fired at the Germans, as sweat poured from his face. The red bandana covering his nose and mouth had fallen down long ago. He believed with all his heart that he'd come to the end of his road.

Chewing his lips and firing his submachine gun, he thought it would be a helluva place to die, in a sewer with dead rats and shit floating by. German bullets zipped over his head and raked the bodies he huddled behind. He wondered if they knew he was all alone. They hadn't shone any flashlights and he thought they weren't very well equipped for what they were trying to do. Their tactics had been very bad. They must be a bunch of assholes. But they outnumbered him and more Germans might show up at any moment. What a fucking mess.

Suddenly the Germans stopped firing.

"SURRENDER!" screamed Colonel Feldheim, who was desperate to capture the men he believed were cowering behind their dead comrades down the tunnel.

Mahoney thought about taking him up on the offer, but he'd heard that POW camps were terrible places. They'd probably kill him anyway once they got him. They might even torture him a little, pull out his fingernails and twist his nose with a pair of pliers.

"FUCK YOU!" he yelled.

"THIS IS OUR LAST OFFER!"

"UP YOUR ASS WITH A TEN-INCH MEAT-HOOK!"

"GET HIM!" shrieked Feldheim.

The Germans charged from behind their cover and Mahoney caught a few of them with a burst from his submachine gun. They dropped into the shit, and the ones who hadn't been hit ducked back behind the walls.

Something told Mahoney that his last chance had arrived. He leapt to his feet, running as fast as he could toward the intersection where Cranepool and Langeais had gone.

Feldheim heard the splashing of feet and realized his quarry was trying to get away. "AFTER HIM!"

The SS men came from behind their cover again, and Mahoney instinctively spun around, dropped to one knee, and gave them another burst. The bullets smacked into Feldheim's chest and cut down two other SS men. The Germans still alive scurried for cover again and Mahoney was on his feet, running like a madman toward the intersection. He dived around it and landed on his stomach in the mush and crap, but he was safe. He scrambled to his feet and dashed to the next intersection, taking a left. Then he ran to the next intersection and took a right. Pausing, he listened and heard the Germans far away. He was loose in labyrinthine passageways of the Cherbourg sewer systems, and he knew that the Germans never would catch him now.

TWENTY-EIGHT

Lieutenant General Lightning Joe Collins sat on his cot and untied his combat boots. It was ten o'clock in the evening and he liked to go to sleep early whenever he could, so that he could get up early in the morning and be ready for anything that might happen. He placed his eyeglasses on the map table near his cot, and rose to blow out the kerosene lamp, when Brigadier General Frank Knowland pushed aside the flap of the tent and entered.

"Sir," said General Knowland, "we've just received word that the German demolition system in Cherbourg has been sabotaged by our Rangers and some of the *maquis*."

Lightning Joe let that sink in for a few moments, then stood and put on his glasses. He looked at his watch and made some quick calculations in his mind. Then he looked at General Knowland, "Our full-scale assault on Cherbourg will begin at midnight. Notify the unit commanders right away."

General Knowland smiled and saluted. "Yes, sir!"

"And have somebody wake up my driver and tell

him to bring my jeep around."

"Yes, sir! Anything else?"

"That will be all for now."

General Knowland turned around and left the tent. Lightning Joe sat on his cot again and began lacing up his boots. He told himself that he must find out who the Rangers were, so he could give them some medals when the battle was over.

TWENTY-NINE

Mahoney, covered from head to foot with dried muck, crept down the Rue Garonne, carrying his submachine gun and looking in all directions. He'd eluded the Germans, come up out of the sewer via a manhole cover on the Boulevard Saint-Denis, and now was on his way back to safety. Artillery barrages of greater intensity than usual were taking place in strategic parts of the city, and he figured that the main American attack probably would come soon.

He descended the three steps in front of the Fleur-de-Lis cafe and opened the door. A handful of people were sipping wine at tables, and Lousteau was reading an old newspaper, having been told that Mahoney and all the others except Cranepool and Soulanges had been killed in the sewer system. Lousteau dropped the newspaper when he recognized Mahoney underneath all the filth. Lousteau jumped to his feet and ran to Mahoney. "It's you!" he said, astonished.

"Who'd you expect?" Mahoney snarled.

Mahoney marched through the kitchen and went

down the stairs to the basement corridor. The door to the meeting room was closed, and he opened it without knocking, stepping inside and slamming the door closed behind him.

Cranepool sat at the round table, a glass of wine in his hand. He didn't drink much as a rule but had got drunk over grief about the fate of Bulldog Boynton, Sergeant Mahoney, Sergeant Newell, and Private Gomez, but especially Sergeant Mahoney, who'd been like a father and big brother combined to him. A few morose Frenchmen also sat at the table.

"Hey, asshole," Mahoney said to Cranepool. "The message get through?"

Cranepool looked up, and his whole body jerked involuntarily, knocking over the glass of wine, when he saw Mahoney. Cranepool didn't know whether to laugh, cry, shit, or go blind.

"I asked you if the message got through," Mahoney repeated, irritation in his voice.

"The message?" Cranepool asked, wondering if he was seeing a ghost.

"Yeah the message. The one to Seventh Corps."

"Um . . . the message got through, Sarge."

Mahoney nodded. "I'm going upstairs to take a bath. If anybody wants me for anything, that's where I'll be, got it?"

"Hup, Sarge," Cranepool said weakly.

Mahoney hung his submachine gun on a peg, and walked out of the room. He climbed the stairs to the top floor, went into the apartment at the end of the hall, staggered to the bathroom, and turned the faucet in the tub. Brown rusty water came out, and after a few seconds it cleared. He put the plug in the hole and took off his clothes, throwing them in a corner. When the tub filled up, Mahoney got in and soaked for a while, then washed himself thoroughly. He pulled the plug and let the water run out of the tub, washed the filthy rings off the walls, and filled it up with water again, climbing in and washing once more.

When he was satisfied that not a speck of the sewer remained anywhere on his body, he left the tub again and looked for a towel to dry himself off with. There were no towels in the bathroom but in the kitchen he found a half pack of cigarettes in a cupboard and lit one with a match that had been lying on the stove. Puffing away, feeling clean and nice again, he went into the bedroom and tore the bedspread off the bed, wrapping himself in it and sitting on a chair near the window.

He felt numb in his mind and exhausted in his body. His eyelids drooped and he looked out the window; Cherbourg was aflame in the distance. He thought of Bulldog Boynton. Old Bulldog had fought in two wars, but finally the bullet had come with his name on it. He hadn't even known what hit him. Probably it was best that way. Mahoney hoped that when the bullet came with his name on it, it would come quick and clean, too.

His eyes narrowed to slits and he thought he'd get some sleep. Stubbing out the cigarette on the floor, he staggered across the room and collapsed on the bed. He crawled up to the pillow and rested his stubbled cheek against it.

In moments he was fast asleep.